Mark Zuckerberg

Shaping Social Media

By Therese Harasymiw

Portions of this book originally appeared in
Mark Zuckerberg by Mary E. Williams.

LUCENT
P R E S S

Published in 2020 by
Lucent Press, an Imprint of Greenhaven Publishing, LLC
353 3rd Avenue
Suite 255
New York, NY 10010

Designer: Deanna Paternostro
Editor: Therese Harasymiw

Library of Congress Cataloging-in-Publication Data

Names: Harasymiw, Therese, author.
Title: Mark Zuckerberg : shaping social media / Therese Harasymiw.
Description: New York : Lucent Press, [2020] | Series: People in the news |
  Includes bibliographical references and index.
Identifiers: LCCN 2018057331 (print) | LCCN 2018059689 (ebook) | ISBN
  9781534567740 (ebook) | ISBN 9781534567733 (pbk. book) | ISBN
  9781534567078 (library bound book)
Subjects: LCSH: Zuckerberg, Mark, 1984– —Juvenile literature. | Facebook
  (Firm)—Juvenile literature. | Facebook (Electronic resource)—Juvenile
  literature. | Online social networks—Juvenile literature. |
  Webmasters—United States—Biography—Juvenile literature. |
  Businessmen—United States—Biography—Juvenile literature.
Classification: LCC HM479.Z83 (ebook) | LCC HM479.Z83 H37 2020 (print) |
DDC
  302.30285 [B]—dc23
LC record available at https://lccn.loc.gov/2018057331

Printed in the United States of America

CPSIA compliance information: Batch #BS19KL: For further information contact Greenhaven Publishing LLC, New York,
New York, at 1-844-317-7404.

Please visit our website, www.greenhavenpublishing.com. For a free color
catalog of all our high-quality books, call toll free 1-844-317-7404 or fax
1-844-317-7405.

Contents

Foreword

We live in a world where the latest news is always available and where it seems we have unlimited access to the lives of the people in the news. Entire television networks are devoted to news about politics, sports, and entertainment. Social media has allowed people to have an unprecedented level of interaction with celebrities. We have more information at our fingertips than ever before. However, how much do we really know about the people we see on television news programs, social media feeds, and magazine covers?

Despite the constant stream of news, the full stories behind the lives of some of the world's most newsworthy men and women are often unknown. Who was Gal Gadot before she became Wonder Woman? What does LeBron James do when he is not playing basketball? What inspires Lin-Manuel Miranda?

This series aims to answer questions like these about some of the biggest names in pop culture, sports, politics, and technology. While the subjects of this series come from all walks of life and areas of expertise, they share a common magnetism that has made them all captivating figures in the public eye. They have shaped the world in some unique way, and—in many cases—they are poised to continue to shape the world for many years to come.

These biographies are not just a collection of basic facts. They tell compelling stories that show how each figure grew to become a powerful public personality. Each book aims to paint a complete, realistic picture of its subject—from the challenges they overcame to the controversies they caused. In doing so, each book reinforces the idea that even the most famous faces on the news are real people who are much more complex than we are often shown in brief video clips or sound bites. Readers are also reminded that there is even more to a person than what they present to the world through social media posts, press releases, and interviews. The whole story of a person's life can only be discovered by digging beneath the surface of their public persona, and that is what this series allows readers to do.

The books in this series are filled with enlightening quotes from speeches and interviews given by the subjects, as well as quotes and anecdotes from those who know their story best: family, friends, coaches, and colleagues. All quotes are noted to provide guidance for further research. Detailed lists of additional resources are also included, as are timelines, indexes, and unique photographs. These text features come together to enhance the reading experience and encourage readers to dive deeper into the stories of these influential men and women.

Fame can be fleeting, but the subjects featured in this series have real staying power. They have fundamentally impacted their respective fields and have achieved great success through hard work and true talent. They are men and women defined by their accomplishments, and they are often seen as role models for the next generation. They have left their mark on the world in a major way, and their stories are meant to inspire readers to leave their mark, too.

Introduction

An Internet Architect

On March 22, 2018, the usually press-shy Mark Zuckerberg sat down for an interview with CNN. The founder of Facebook addressed the controversy that had hit Facebook that year: a political consulting business called Cambridge Analytica had used Facebook to acquire data from millions of users, in violation of Facebook policies. People were furious that the social network had allowed this information leak to happen. Zuckerberg publicly apologized and promised the security team would redouble their efforts to stop data breaches. He regretted it occurred, going on to admit:

> I've made every kind of mistake that you can make. I mean I started this when I was so young and inexperienced, right? I made technical errors and business errors. I hired the wrong people. I trusted the wrong people. I've probably launched more products that have failed than most people will in their lifetime.[1]

This was an honest admission from a man once called the "boy wonder" of the tech industry. Many just know him as a billionaire who laid the groundwork for his success without even graduating from college. To them, Zuckerberg has had it easy:

He was born with keen intelligence, had the opportunities to attend the finest schools, and stumbled on the right connections to strike it big in Silicon Valley.

However, Zuckerberg's story is not so simple. It is true that he came upon the idea for Facebook while at Harvard University. But he had several stops and starts until he honed a winning idea. In fact, one of his earlier schemes, a website called Facemash, nearly got him expelled. That fiasco contained the seed of an idea that catapulted Zuckerberg into another project: creating an online and interactive version of photo directories that on-campus students received at the beginning of the school year, nicknamed "facebooks." He launched a network, then known as Thefacebook, from his dorm room on February 4, 2004. It would revolutionize social media relatively quickly. Zuckerberg and his friends kept the fledgling company alive with their own money, sleepless nights of work, and a few agonizing decisions. Some of those decisions Zuckerberg would regret, but all would make Facebook the powerful enterprise it is today.

Transforming Technology

Facebook transformed from a bare-bones website used by a few Ivy League students in 2004 to a sophisticated public net-working platform with more than 2 billion global members. It is the most visited social network in the world, and it has made Zuckerberg, with an estimated $56 billion in personal wealth, one of the youngest multibillionaires in the world.

Yet Zuckerberg never set out to run a company and become immensely wealthy. He maintains that he simply loves writing computer code and making technological tools that help peo-ple learn, share, and connect more with each other. As such, he sees himself—and Facebook—as expressing the spirit of his generation, which was shaped by the information revolution of the late 20th century. Zuckerberg explained in an interview:

Facebook's superstar founder was once a college student with a simple idea about connecting people online.

I'm in the first generation of people who really grew up with the internet. Google came out when I was in middle school. Then there was Amazon and Wikipedia and iTunes and Napster. Each year, there were new ways to access information. Now you can look up anything you want. Now you can get cool reference material. Now you can download any song you want. Now you can get directions to anything. The world kept on getting better and better.[2]

Zuckerberg is a shining example of an optimist. He has said that Facebook's purpose is to connect the world, and he believes that values such as empathy, accountability, and integrity emerge naturally when people are given more ways to share and relate to each other. The past, in contrast, offered fewer opportunities for these values to find expression. "If you go back, most people in the world had no voice, or they had no podium where they could share things. But now everyone does,"[3] Zuckerberg said.

Not everyone agrees that Zuckerberg simply wants to build bridges between people. Former colleagues accused him of stealing the idea for Facebook from their social network. Privacy advocates question Facebook's motives for tracking users' web-surfing habits and using that information to benefit advertisers and other interested parties. A 2010 movie depicting the founding of Facebook painted Zuckerberg as an envious nerd driven by the need to prove himself to the cool crowd. Zuckerberg resents this portrayal: "[The moviemakers] just can't wrap their head around the idea that someone might build something because they like building things."[4]

The Go-To Tech Tool

Undeniably, Zuckerberg's delight in building tools has transformed how people communicate with each other. Today, many people prefer Facebook to email as a way to contact friends and family online. Others use it to share photos, videos, music, and links to news stories, editorials, blogs, or other sites. Most users log in at least once a day to write updates, see what their friends are up to, converse with members of a group, play games, or send messages. Maybe that is why, even with controversies like the Cambridge Analytica scandal, members usually do not quit Facebook.

In 2010, Zuckerberg suggested, "I think, if anything, the Facebook story is a great example of how, if you're building a product that people love, you can make a lot of mistakes."[5] To many, there is no other social network available that offers such a variety of easily accessible ways to connect and communicate with others.

Facebook is the most popular social network around the world. People as young as 13 can join.

Zuckerberg is the first to admit that he never thought he would be the one behind such a world-changing business. He remembers dreaming with friends about such an endeavor, but he said, "We were nineteen years old, we were in college, we knew *nothing* about companies. . . . Who'd have thought it, right?"[6]

Chapter **One**

Growing Up Zuckerberg

Mark Elliot Zuckerberg was born on May 14, 1984, at a hospital in White Plains, New York, to Edward and Karen Zuckerberg. They lived in the nearby village of Dobbs Ferry, New York, in the prosperous suburban county of Westchester, just north of New York City.

At the time of Mark's birth, he had one older sister, Randi, but more Zuckerberg children were on the way. Mark, the sole boy among four siblings, also has two younger sisters: Donna and Arielle. The children were told they could be anything they wanted to be, but they should try their best at whatever they pursued. The Zuckerberg household was a perfect atmosphere for an inquisitive young child like Mark to grow up in.

An Encouraging Upbringing

Mark's father, Ed, ran a dental practice in the basement of the family's large house. Karen left her job as a psychiatrist after the birth of the couple's first child and became a stay-at-home mom and an office manager for her husband's practice.

Ed had grown up as the son of a Brooklyn, New York, mail carrier whose "method of fixing a TV that went out of whack was to take a fist and pop it,"[7] according to Mark. Ed took an entirely

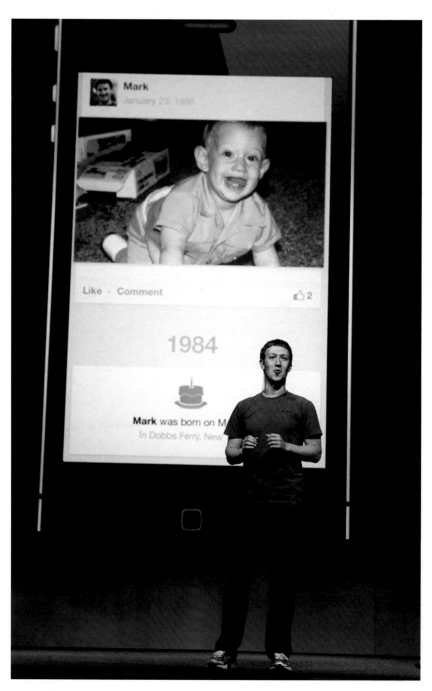

Zuckerberg has always been close with his family. Here, he is shown with a picture of himself as a child.

different approach to modern equipment as a teen: He enjoyed taking stereos apart just to see how they worked.

Mark had the same curious, analytical nature that his father had displayed in his own youth. Ed described Mark as "strong-willed and relentless" as a young boy. While many young children are satisfied with yes or no answers to their questions, "if [Mark] asked for something, *yes* by itself would work, but *no* required much more," Ed remembered. "If you were going to say no to him, you had better be prepared with a strong argument backed by facts, experiences, logic, reasons. We envisioned him becoming a lawyer one day, with a near 100% success rate of convincing juries."[8]

Ed and Karen Zuckerberg are proud of their son's accomplishments. Ed has jokingly called himself "literally the father of Facebook."

The Zuckerbergs were strongly committed to encouraging their children to develop their particular talents and to follow their dreams. "Rather than impose upon your kids or try and steer their lives in a certain direction, … support the development of the things they're passionate about,"[9] Ed said. Mark's talent for out-of-the-box thinking emerged early in a supportive household that valued education, skill, and creativity.

Concentrating on Computers

Mark's analytical skills eventually became focused on computers and technology. The first Macintosh Apple computer was launched in 1984, the year Mark was born. That same year, his father purchased his first office computer, a huge IBM XT. Although it did little more than print out invoices, Ed relished it: "It wasn't about the math; it was about the vision."[10]

By 1985, the entire Zuckerberg home and office were computerized. Ed himself had a limited background in computer science, but he enjoyed acquiring the latest technological gadgets for his practice as well as for recreation. All four of the Zuckerberg children were given their own computers. This proved to be a boon for Mark, who had become bored with his schoolwork. "There are advantages to being exposed to computers early on," Ed noted. "That certainly enriched Mark's interest in technology."[11]

Among the high-tech devices that Ed bought was an early Atari 800, one of the first home computers. Resembling a large electric typewriter, the machine came with a disk that enabled Mark to learn a version of BASIC (Beginner's All-purpose Symbolic Instruction Code), a computer programming language. The Zuckerbergs also gave Mark the book *C++ for Dummies*, an introduction to programming. When he was nearly 11 years old, Mark's parents hired David Newman, a software developer, to tutor Mark at home once a week. "He was a prodigy," Newman claimed. "Sometimes it was tough to stay ahead of him."[12]

In addition to Newman's tutoring, Mark began attending graduate computer courses at nearby Mercy College once a week. Mark's young age was a surprise to his classmates and his teachers there. When Ed dropped him off for his first class, the instructor looked at Ed and said, motioning to Mark, "You can't bring him to the classroom with you."[13] Ed had to explain that it was the boy who was taking the class.

ZuckNet

Early on, Mark had inventive skills and a penchant for creating tools to get things done faster. One day in 1996, when Mark was almost 12, he heard his father say that he wished there were a better way of announcing a patient's arrival than having the receptionist yell down from upstairs. Using the Atari BASIC computer language, Mark created a messaging software program that enabled all the Zuckerberg home and office computers to communicate with each other. The family named it "ZuckNet." Professionals were brought in to do the wiring of ZuckNet, as home computer networks were basically unheard of at that time. ZuckNet was, in essence, a primitive version of America Online's (AOL's) Instant Messenger, which did not come out until the following year.

Fantasy, Fun, and Games

Mark's taste for computers and other new gadgets also had a dreamy, playful side. His favorite movies were the first three *Star Wars* films (Episodes IV, V, and VI). This science fiction and fantasy series is full of special effects and visionary technologies. One year, during a wintertime school break, Mark and his sisters decided to film a complete parody of *Star Wars*. They named it *The Star Wars Sill-ogy*. "We took our job very seriously," his sister Randi said. "Every morning we'd wake up and have production meetings. Mark's voice hadn't changed yet, so he played [the protagonist] Luke Skywalker with a really high, squeaky voice, and then my little sister, who I think was 2, we stuck her in a garbage can as [robot] R2-D2 and had her walk around."[14] When he turned 13, Mark had a bar mitzvah ceremony, a coming-of-age ceremony for Jewish boys. His party had a *Star Wars* theme.

Pranks and practical jokes were a part of life in the Zuckerberg home. One night, Mark's sister Donna was working on her computer in her room downstairs. Mark turned to Randi and said, "I bet I can make Donna come upstairs in five seconds."[15] He rigged things so that a screen popped up on Donna's computer, warning her that she had downloaded a virus that would cause the computer to self-destruct in 30 seconds. The machine began counting down, and up the stairs Donna ran, yelling for Mark. Later, in 1999, the Zuckerberg parents were, like much of the computer-using world at the time, worried about the Y2K (Year 2000) bug, a potential massive failure among computers that many feared would occur when the year rolled over from 1999 to 2000. One main concern was that there might be widespread blackouts. As a prank on New Year's Eve 1999, Mark and Randi waited until the stroke of midnight—then secretly shut off the electrical power to the house.

Twenty-first century technologies held great appeal for Mark's circle of friends. Many of them loved to play computer games. Mark went further: He loved to write programming code for computer games. He created a version of the board game Monopoly—with his middle school as the setting—as well as a variation on the board game Risk. "It was centered around the ancient Roman Empire," Mark explained. "You played against Julius Caesar. He was good, and I was never able to win."[16] Mark also gained inspiration for coding from friends of his who were artists. He could build a game around their sketches.

From Public to Private

For much of his childhood, Mark attended local public schools. He enrolled at Ardsley High School, a place not far from his home, where he excelled in classics: the languages, history, and culture of ancient Greece and ancient Rome. As well as he did at

Randi Zuckerberg would later become the director of market development for Facebook, but she left in 2011 to start a social media business called Zuckerberg Media.

Ardsley, however, Mark transferred to Phillips Exeter Academy, an elite private school, after his sophomore year. Ardsley did not offer many computer or higher math courses, and Mark's parents wanted to boost his chances of being admitted to an Ivy League college.

Phillips Exeter provided a more challenging environment for an eager and inventive mind like Mark's. His required coursework included art, classical and modern languages, computer science, math, health and human development, history, religion, and science. Mark won prizes in math, astronomy, and physics; he also

Phillips Exeter Academy is located in Exeter, New Hampshire. It has about 1,085 students.

excelled in literature, classics, and Latin. He jokingly claimed that he preferred Latin and other ancient languages only because he spoke modern foreign languages with such a poor accent. However, he later explained that he was drawn to Latin in particular because he likened it to a coding language in his mind. He could read and write Latin in the same way he could read and write code. Additionally, he had always been fascinated with the powerful historical figures of ancient Rome, especially the emperor Augustus Caesar. Mark made tentative plans to study classics at Harvard after finishing high school. Phillips Exeter's highly regarded Latin program would provide a strong foundation for college-level classics.

An Elite Academy

Established in 1781, Phillips Exeter Academy is a boarding school for boys and girls located in rural New Hampshire. Phillips Exeter is noted for using the Harkness method, a seminar style of learning in which eight to twelve students sit around a large, oval table with a teacher who instructs them through conferences and tutorials, encouraging each person to actively participate. There are no lectures, no traditional textbooks, and no classrooms containing rows of desks. Approaches to teaching different subjects vary, but the main goal is to have students come up with ideas of their own and to practice good critical-thinking and discussion skills. In some cases, teachers hardly speak at all, interjecting only to guide the class discussion. Famous Phillips Exeter alumni include U.S. president Franklin Pierce, U.S. senator Jay Rockefeller, businessperson Joseph Coors, and the authors Gore Vidal and John Irving.

Beyond the Classroom

Mark's achievements and experiences during his time at Exeter extended beyond the academic. He played in the school band. In addition, after being voted 2000's most valuable player at the New York regional competition of the U.S. Fencing Association (USFA), Mark became captain of the Exeter fencing team. He saw fencing as "the perfect medium" because "whether I am competing against a rival in a USFA tournament or just clashing foils [fencing swords], or sometimes sabers, with a friend, I rarely find myself doing anything more enjoyable than fencing a good bout."[17] Still, Mark continued toying with inventive projects to challenge his mind, creating new conveniences for the people around him. With his classmate Kristopher Tillery, for example, he set up a website that allowed Exeter students to order snacks online.

Mark's time at prep school also exposed him to a lifestyle that emphasized strong social ties with his peers. As writer Steffan Antonas noted, "Exeter's tight-knit boarding community lives on campus full-time. Students refer to themselves as 'Exonians' and have a strong group identity rooted in a rich culture of customs and tradition."[18] For many years, part of this tradition included receiving an annual edition of the school's student directory. When Mark enrolled at Phillips Exeter at the beginning of his junior year, he and all the other students were given a copy of this directory. Its cover title was "The Photo Address Book," but students referred to it as "the Facebook."

As the name suggests, Phillips Exeter's "Facebook" contained the name, photograph, campus house address, and contact information of each student. Such photo directories were (and still are) a significant part of social life at many prep schools. With cell phones banned on campus, hundreds of students leaving and arriving annually, and students' living accommodations changing from year to year, the school's Facebook was a well-appreciated and necessary resource. As Antonas pointed out, "Not only do students need the directory to find and contact their peers, but the books become part of the culture of bonding between classmates and friends, as students use it to see where their peers live, who's hot and who's not, who lives with who, and who the new kids are."[19]

In 2002, when Mark was a senior, the student council successfully lobbied the school administration to launch an online version of the Phillips Exeter Facebook. Mark was not involved with this development, however. His attention was increasingly drawn to innovative computer programming experiments. Phillips Exeter's Computer Science Division invited students to rethink their views about how technology can be used in the world. They were encouraged to consider what computers could do and not focus on what they cannot do. In other words, they could get creative with technology. Accordingly, Mark embarked on an ambitious senior project with his classmate and friend Adam D'Angelo.

The Synapse Project

For their senior project, Mark and Adam formed a company they named Intelligent Media Group and created Synapse Media Player, a software program that was able to build a digital music list based on a user's musical tastes. Mark explained, "It learned your listening patterns by figuring out how much you like each song at a given point of time, and which songs you tend to listen to around each other."[20] The program calculated the probability of the listener wanting to listen to a certain song. He and Adam posted about Synapse on Slashdot, a website concerned with technology, and offered it as a free download. Mark believed that the software should belong to everyone. It was important to him that it remained free for anyone who wanted to use it. News about the groundbreaking software spread quickly, and it was given mostly positive reviews by music technology users.

Soon, several large companies, including Microsoft, expressed an interest in recruiting Mark and Adam and in purchasing Synapse. One offered close to $1 million and a job for three years. But the young entrepreneurs turned the offers down, opting to attend college instead. They bought the patent for their product and hoped that they had made the right decision. Later, when they were in college, they decided they wanted to sell Synapse,

Adam D'Angelo (left), Zuckerberg's high school friend, would later serve as chief technology officer of Facebook, but he left in 2008 to found a question-and-answer website called Quora.

but it was too late by then. No one was interested in buying Synapse. This was an early business lesson for Adam and Mark.

In the spring of 2002, Mark graduated from Phillips Exeter with a diploma in classics. By all accounts, he was a well-rounded student. He could read and write French, Hebrew, Latin, and ancient Greek. He was a fencing champion, a math whiz, and a skilled computer programmer. Mark was accepted by Harvard University. He moved to the prestigious school's Cambridge, Massachusetts, campus in the autumn of 2002, ready for the next chapter in his life.

Chapter **Two**

Hacking at Harvard

Mark Zuckerberg arrived at Harvard in fall 2002. He decided to major in psychology, his mother's career field, as well as computer science, which was clearly his passion. Initially, Zuckerberg did not really stand out in a crowd of his peers. At one of the country's most elite universities, he was surrounded by hundreds of bright freshmen who were also talented and ambitious. At 5 feet 7 inches (170 cm), with a slender build, freckled face, and curly brown hair, he appeared a little younger than his 18 years. He tended to wear baggy jeans, rubber flip-flops—even in winter—and T-shirts with witty phrases or images.

Zuckerberg might not have been physically imposing, but it did not take long for his programming skills to catch the eye of his fellow Ivy Leaguers. He quickly exhibited that he had a talent for crafting simple software applications that people wanted to use.

More to Mark

As an introvert and a deliberate thinker, Zuckerberg tended to be quiet around strangers. According to author David Kirkpatrick, however, this quietness was deceiving:

When he did speak, he was wry. His tendency was to say noth-ing until others fully had their say. He stared. He would stare at you while you were talking, and stay absolutely silent. If you said something stimulating, he'd finally fire up his own ideas and the words would come cascading out. But if you went on too long or said something obvious, he would start looking through you. When you finished, he'd quietly mutter "yeah," then change the subject or turn away.[21]

Zuckerberg seemed to embrace a standoffish, geeky person-ality, but he also enjoyed parties. He joined the Jewish frater-nity, Alpha Epsilon Pi. At one of their Friday night parties, he met the woman who would later become his wife, Priscilla Chan. As they stood in a line outside of the restroom, the two chatted. "He was this nerdy guy who was just a little bit out there," Chan recalled. "I remember he had these beer glasses that said 'pound include beer dot H.' It's a tag for C++. It's like college humor but with a nerdy, computer-science appeal."[22]

Underneath a distant exterior, Zuckerberg was full of ideas, self-confidence, and mischief. During his stint at Harvard, his brilliance and persistence would bring him recognition even as his occasional misbehavior got him into trouble.

Dorm Life

At the beginning of his sophomore year, Zuckerberg was living in one of the smallest four-person suites in Kirkland House, a Harvard dorm. Each suite contained two bedrooms joined by a common room, where all four suitemates had their own work desk. Zuckerberg was rooming with Chris Hughes, a history and literature major interested in public policy. Dustin Moskovitz, an economics major, and Billy Olson, who was involved in theater, lived in the other half of the suite.

About Harvard

Established in 1636, Harvard University is the oldest institution of higher education in the United States. Harvard College, its undergraduate school, has an average of 6,700 students each year. Freshmen live in one of the Harvard Yard dormitories. After completing their first year, students reside in one of the 12 houses on campus, guided by a resident master and staff of tutors. Ninety-seven percent of undergrads live on campus, creating a strong sense of campus community. The college boasts numerous famous graduates, such as U.S. president John F. Kennedy, cellist Yo-Yo Ma, and actress Natalie Portman. It also has some well-known dropouts, including actor Matt Damon, Microsoft founder Bill Gates, and Mark Zuckerberg.

This photograph shows the part of Harvard University called Harvard Yard.

Zuckerberg's dorm, Kirkland House, is pictured here.

The bedrooms were designed to fit bunk beds and one small desk. Zuckerberg and Hughes, deciding that neither of them wanted to sleep on the top bunk, dismantled the beds so that they each rested on the floor. This left them very little room, given that the desk was typically loaded with papers and trash. The entire suite was always messy. Zuckerberg had a habit of leaving food wrappers and empty cans and bottles all over the place. Sometimes Moskovitz's girlfriend got tired of the clutter and threw out the trash. Once, when Zuckerberg's mother was visiting, she apologized to Moskovitz for her son's untidiness, explaining he had been cared for by a nanny as a boy.

In the midst of this clutter was Zuckerberg's 8-foot-long (2.4 m) whiteboard, which he used for brainstorming ideas and writing out formulas. The only place it fit was along the wall in the hallway between the bedrooms. "He really loved that whiteboard," Moskovitz recalled. "He always wanted to draw out his ideas, even when that didn't necessarily make them clearer."[23] In contrast to his messiness, Zuckerberg's handwriting was painstakingly neat and tiny. He sometimes filled up entire notebooks with extensive reflections.

Engrossed with Ideas

Zuckerberg was brimming with ideas for new internet services. He spent many hours writing code, often going without sleep and neglecting his homework in his non–computer science classes. On most nights, he was found at his desk in the common room, hunched over his computer, exploring new ways to share information. He and his suitemates generally got along well, and they became involved with each other's projects.

Computer programming and the internet were recurring topics of interest for the four young men. Zuckerberg and Moskovitz had ongoing friendly debates about website features and how the internet might evolve as its number of users increased. Hughes, who initially had no interest in computers, became intrigued with the discussions and began sharing his opinions, as did Olson. Zuckerberg dreamed up new programming projects, and the other three men offered their suggestions on how to develop them. "I had like twelve projects that year," said Zuckerberg. "Of course I wasn't fully committed to any one of them." Most of them focused on "seeing how people were connected through mutual references."[24]

During the first week of his sophomore year, Zuckerberg created Course Match, a program that helped Harvard students choose classes based on the selections of other students. As Zuckerberg put it, the new program was a way of "link[ing] to people through things."[25] Course Match was instantly popular, and hundreds of students began using it. He ran the program from his dorm room laptop computer, and it eventually crashed because of the high demand.

Later that school year, Zuckerberg created an online community study guide for his art history course. Having barely attended the class all semester, he needed a way to cram for the final exam. He compiled a series of images from the course and emailed other class members, inviting them to contribute to the study guide by adding comments next to the images. After spending an evening reading their notes, he passed the exam.

A Professor's Opinion

Harvard University computer science professor Harry Lewis taught both Microsoft founder Bill Gates and Facebook creator Mark Zuckerberg. He maintains that Gates and Zuckerberg shared a similar approach to learning when they were college students:

> The thing I would say about Zuckerberg is that he was very eager to learn and very skeptical about whether anything we were teaching him was actually the right thing for him to be learning. I think Bill Gates had exactly the same feeling. It was not disrespect for what was being taught, but maybe [it was] not exactly what he was interested in ... so he was ... absorbing everything and not paying any attention to it at the same time.[1]

1. Quoted in CNBC, *Mark Zuckerberg: Inside Facebook*, Documentary, January 26, 2011.

Sophomore-Year Scandal

The most notorious program Zuckerberg devised, however, was the one that came together during the fall semester of 2003. It introduced a rebellious, mischievous side of Zuckerberg. The purpose of the program, named Facemash, was to rate a student's attractiveness. A user was invited to compare pictures of two students of the same gender and vote on which one was "hotter." As a student's rating went up, he or she would be compared to others who had been rated hotter, until the "hottest" was chosen.

Zuckerberg began creating the new program on Tuesday evening, October 28, after he had an argument with a young woman. He wrote about it in his blog, titling his entries "Harvard Face Mash: The Process." He insulted the girl and wrote, "I need to think of something to make to take my mind off her. I need to think of something to occupy my mind."[26]

Zuckerberg occupied himself by looking at student pictures in the Kirkland House online facebook, a who's who of people in his dorm similar to the book he had at Phillips Exeter. Each Harvard dorm maintained this kind of student directory, which listed the names of all its students alongside their photos. The photos were of poor quality, similar to the kind of pictures on driver's licenses, and were taken the day students arrived for orientation. "I'm a little intoxicated, not gonna lie. So what?" wrote Zuckerberg of that night. "The Kirkland facebook is open on my computer desktop and some of these people have pretty horrendous facebook pics."[27]

Through the rest of that night, Zuckerberg found ways to download the digital facebooks of nine of Harvard's twelve houses. A friend at Lowell House gave Zuckerberg temporary use of his password. At another dorm, Zuckerberg physically snuck in to download data from an ethernet cable he plugged into the wall. Most of the time, he simply hacked in over the internet and continued to blog about his adventure.

Zuckerberg's initial impulse was to compare each student to a picture of a farm animal. It was his suitemate Billy Olson who suggested comparing each person with another person and only occasionally including a farm animal. By the time most of the preliminary data had been downloaded—by 4:00 a.m., according to Zuckerberg's blog—the animal pictures had been dropped.

Facemash Debut and Finale

Zuckerberg took a few more days to write the algorithms—complex mathematical programs—to make the website work. When the site was nearly completed, Zuckerberg seemed to recognize that the project might get him in trouble. He wrote in his blog, "Perhaps Harvard will squelch [Facemash] for legal reasons. … But one thing is certain, and it's that I'm a jerk for making this site. Oh well. Someone had to do it eventually."[28] He launched Facemash on the afternoon of Sunday, November 2.

Zuckerberg emailed the link to his new site to a few friends, wanting to test it out. Those friends then forwarded the link to other friends, including those in other dorms and on various student email lists. Traffic skyrocketed. Within a few hours, the site had logged 450 visitors and 22,000 votes. Around 10:00 p.m., when Zuckerberg returned to his room after a meeting, Facemash was so flooded with users that he could not log on to his own computer.

The site was an immediate underground hit, but not everyone was happy with Zuckerberg's mischief. Complaints of sexism and racism spread among members of two campus women's groups—Fuerza Latina and the Association of Black Harvard Women. Harvard's computer services department traced the source of Facemash to Zuckerberg's computer and shut off his web access.

Facing the Consequences

Zuckerberg emailed apology letters to Fuerza Latina and the Association of Black Harvard Women, explaining that he had only intended to conduct an experiment and get a few friends' opinions on it. He said he did not know how quickly news of the site would spread and the consequences that would come of it. However, he stated, he understood how others could have misunderstood his intentions in building it. In a November 4, 2003, interview and article in the *Harvard Crimson* campus newspaper, Zuckerberg claimed he never expected to gain such widespread publicity and that he had decided to shut Facemash down for good: "The primary concern is hurting people's feelings. I'm not willing to risk insulting anyone."[29]

On November 18, 2003, Zuckerberg appeared before Harvard's disciplinary administrative board. Joining him at the hearing were his suitemate Billy Olson, who had contributed ideas to the Facemash project; the student who had given Zuckerberg the Lowell House password; and Joe Green, a dorm neighbor who had also helped out. Zuckerberg was charged with breach of security, copyright infringement, and violation of privacy. He apologized but also suggested that he had done Harvard a favor by revealing the security vulnerabilities of the sites he had so easily hacked. The deans were not pleased by this justification, but they decided not to expel Zuckerberg and placed him on probation instead.

After the hearing, Zuckerberg celebrated his relatively light punishment by sharing a bottle of champagne with his Kirkland neighbors and seemed not to care much that he had narrowly avoided big trouble. Green's father was, by chance, visiting his son on the night of this celebration. "My dad was trying to drill it into Mark's head that this was really a big deal, that he'd almost gotten suspended," Green recalled. "But Mark didn't want to hear it. My dad came away with the notion that I shouldn't do any more Zuckerberg projects."[30]

New Connections

For others, however, the Facemash stunt was proof that Zuckerberg had a flair for making software that people loved to use, and many were eager to collaborate with him. Occasionally, he worked on other people's projects. Wanting to make up for the offense caused by Facemash, for example, he helped the Association of Black Harvard Women set up its own website.

In November 2003, he was approached by three senior students—twins Cameron and Tyler Winklevoss and their friend Divya Narendra—who were building a student socializing website they called Harvard Connection. The site would have two sections, "Dating" and "Connecting," where students could post pictures of themselves along with some personal information. Narendra and the Winklevoss twins had started constructing Harvard Connection in December 2002, hiring some students to write code for it, but at the end of 2003, it remained unfinished. After reading about the Facemash episode in the campus newspaper, the three wanted Zuckerberg to do the programming for Harvard Connection. He agreed to help them out.

According to Narendra and the Winklevoss brothers, Zuckerberg initially seemed excited about their project. On the day after their first meeting, Zuckerberg sent them an email saying he would be able to set up Harvard Connection fairly quickly. He did some work on the project, but as the weeks passed, Zuckerberg apparently lost interest. Narendra and the Winklevosses contended that Zuckerberg promised to do more work but kept postponing meeting with them, claiming that his schedule was keeping him too busy.

An Online Directory

Part of what was keeping Zuckerberg busy was a project of his own that he started during the winter break. According to Zuckerberg, this new project was largely inspired by editorials about Facemash in the *Harvard Crimson*. One editorial suggested that students might wish to share their photos and personal information with a community of their own choosing. Other *Crimson* articles expressed a popular sentiment among Harvard students at the time: that the university should take the photo directories—the facebooks—maintained by each house, combine them, and make them available online in searchable form.

Students at other colleges were pushing for the same thing. New interactive services, such as Friendster and MySpace, had recently sprouted up on the internet. Students were eager to see campus-focused websites where they could search for others according to their interests and create an online network of friends.

Encouraged by the Harvard community's desire for an online directory, Zuckerberg combined elements from two of

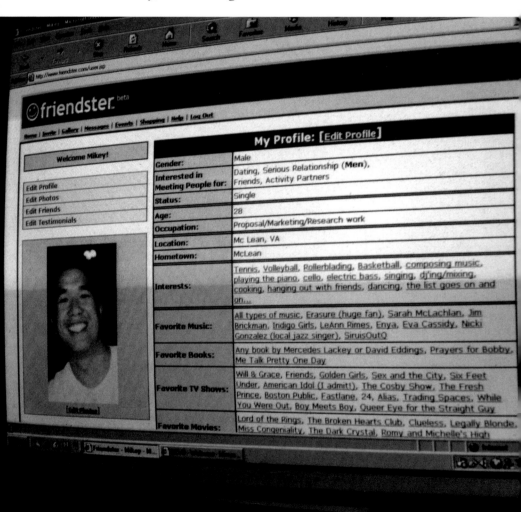

Friendster was an early competitor of Facebook's. It later became a social gaming site, but it finally dissolved as a company.

his previous projects—Course Match and Facemash—with ideas borrowed from Friendster. The result was a new website, founded on January 11, 2004, when Zuckerberg officially registered a web address as thefacebook.com. Thefacebook was to serve as an online communications tool and directory that would enable students to share information and keep track of their classmates. While Friendster was seen mainly as a dating site, Zuckerberg initially saw Thefacebook strengthening connections that already existed.

In the meantime, the creators of Harvard Connection were still waiting to hear about Zuckerberg's progress on their website. Cameron Winklevoss emailed Zuckerberg on January 6, and Zuckerberg apologized by email two days later, again claiming that he was swamped with homework and programming projects. Finally, he met with Narendra and the Winklevosses on January 14 and told them that they needed to find another programmer for their site.

Introducing Thefacebook

On that day, the three Harvard Connection partners had no idea that Zuckerberg had officially registered a website that was to serve as an online network for the university. Nor did they know that on January 12, Zuckerberg had contacted his fraternity brother, a business-savvy junior named Eduardo Saverin, to discuss marketing strategies for Thefacebook. After his experiences with Course Match and Facemash—which both had caused his computer to crash—Zuckerberg knew he needed to find a larger server to host Thefacebook. Moreover, since he had gotten in trouble with Harvard's administration board over Facemash, he wanted a server that was not affiliated with Harvard. With the help of a hosting site, he found a suitable place to store Thefacebook's software and data. Zuckerberg and Saverin each invested $1,000 to help pay the monthly fees for the server. Saverin was given ownership of 30 percent of Thefacebook in exchange for his investment and business advice.

On February 4, Thefacebook went live. In an article in the *Harvard Crimson*, Zuckerberg admitted that he had

Chris Hughes (right) was a spokesman for Facebook until 2007, when he left to campaign for future president Barack Obama.

worn himself out getting the network started: "If I hadn't launched it that day, I was about to just can it and go on to the next thing."[31] His hard work bore fruit. The first users of Thefacebook, Zuckerberg's Kirkland neighbors, sent emails to other students asking them to join. This led to yet more invitations to an increasing number of friends, with dozens signing up right away. By the fifth day after launch, about 1,000 students had joined, and Thefacebook had become a main topic of conversation at meals and between classes.

Part of the appeal of Thefacebook was its exclusivity and its privacy controls. Only people with a Harvard email address could sign up, and profiles included a single photo with a user's real name along with other personal information the user was willing to share. Users were also able to set their privacy options to limit who could see their information—perhaps just current students or only people in their own dormitory. Zuckerberg had a personal reason for creating these features. As a *Crimson* article pointed out, he "hoped the privacy options would help to restore his reputation following student outrage over facemash.com."[32] These features also distinguished Thefacebook from other social networks, such as Friendster and MySpace.

By the end of its first three weeks, Thefacebook had more than 6,000 users. Zuckerberg, realizing that he needed more help to operate the website, enlisted his suitemates. He hired Dustin Moskovitz as vice president of programming, while Chris Hughes became director of publicity. The team's first priority, Zuckerberg insisted, would be to add more colleges to the network. He brought in California Institute of Technology student Adam D'Angelo, his inventing buddy from high school, to help set up databases at other universities.

Controversy

The arrival of Thefacebook infuriated Zuckerberg's former Harvard Connection partners. They claimed Zuckerberg stole their idea and postponed work on their site on purpose so he could launch his site before theirs. In an interview with the *Harvard Crimson*, Cameron Winklevoss said that Zuckerberg "boasted about completing [Thefacebook] in a week, after leading us on for three months. We passed through Thanksgiving, winter break and intersession. He had ample time. He not only led us on, but he knew what he was doing."[33]

Zuckerberg argued that the idea of a social network was not novel: "There aren't very many new ideas floating around," he told the *Crimson*. "The facebook isn't even a very novel idea. It's taken from all these others ... And ours was that we're going to do it on the level of schools."[34]

Later, however, evidence was found that proved the Harvard Connection partners at least partly correct. Zuckerberg had been leading them on. In an instant message sent in December 2003, Zuckerberg had written to a friend about Harvard Connection: "They made a mistake haha. They asked me to make it for them. So I'm like delaying it so it won't be ready until after the facebook thing comes out."[35]

The Winklevosses sent a letter to Zuckerberg, demanding that he shut down Thefacebook or else they would charge him with breaking the school's honor code. They met with Harvard president Lawrence Summers, hoping he would take action against Zuckerberg. In response, Zuckerberg sent his own letter to administrators defending himself: "Frankly, I'm kind of appalled that they're threatening me after the work I've done for them free of charge." He added, "I try to shrug it off as a minor annoyance that whenever I do something successful, every capitalist out there wants a piece of the action."[36] After reading the Winklevosses' complaint and Zuckerberg's response, Summers decided that the matter was beyond the university's authority. The Harvard Connection team sought legal advice off campus.

Meanwhile, Thefacebook continued to attract new users. By the end of March 2004, it had expanded to several more universities, including Columbia, Stanford, and Yale, and the number of active users exceeded 30,000. On April 13, Eduardo Saverin, calling himself the chief financial officer of the company, officially made Thefacebook a business by setting it up as a limited liability company (LLC) in Florida, his state of residence. Mark Zuckerberg irreverently posted his own job description as: "Founder, Master and Commander, and Enemy of the State."[37]

Chapter Three

The Foundations of Facebook

By the time Mark Zuckerberg's sophomore year at Harvard was ending in May 2004, Thefacebook had 200,000 users at about 30 schools. It was not the only social networking site at some of these campuses, but it took hold wherever it was introduced. The team worked hard to establish Thefacebook on campuses before other social networks, obtaining student email lists and getting the word out. At some schools, such as Stanford University in California, a majority of the entire student body signed up within just 24 hours of the site's launch. Soon, schools were asking for Thefacebook.

Success meant a lot more work for the young businessmen, though. The growing number of users taxed the website and the five servers on which it relied. Zuckerberg and Dustin Moskovitz, in particular, had to tinker with the site to make it stay afloat. Moskowitz basically learned on the job about programming. This was all while the young men were trying not to fail out of school.

Eduardo Saverin persuaded Zuckerberg that they needed an influx of cash that was not their own. They could get this by letting businesses run ads on the site. Zuckerberg agreed, but his reluctance was clearly visible. The initial advertisements ran with text near it that said: "We don't like these either but they pay the bills."[38]

Dustin Moscovitz and Zuckerberg are pictured here at Harvard. Moscovitz continued to work for Facebook until 2008.

The advertising firm Y2M, interested in selling ads on Thefacebook, suggested that the site's traffic data—its number of users and the amount it was used—must have been incorrect because the numbers were so high. Y2M was thrilled to find out the data was indeed accurate. What remained to be seen was whether the social network would turn out to be profitable for all involved.

Connecting with Sean Parker

One well-known developer from California's Silicon Valley, Sean Parker, heard about Thefacebook when it became a hit on the Stanford campus. Parker had helped to build Napster, an online music file-sharing service, and cofounded Plaxo, an online address book and network. Excited about Thefacebook's potential, Parker contacted Zuckerberg and offered to connect him with investors in California.

Parker flew to New York City in early April 2004, where he met Saverin, Zuckerberg, and their girlfriends for dinner at a fashionable Chinese restaurant. Zuckerberg, enthusiastic about the kinds of innovations Napster had accomplished, was delighted to meet Parker. Likewise, Parker was impressed with Zuckerberg's brilliance and ambition. The two fell into an intense dialogue about what Thefacebook might become. As Parker recalled, Zuckerberg "was not thinking, 'Let's make some money and get out.' This wasn't like a get-rich-quick scheme. This was 'Let's build something that has lasting cultural value and try to take over the world.' But he didn't know what that meant. Taking over the world meant taking over college."[39]

By the end of May 2004, Thefacebook did appear to be taking over prestigious colleges, having conquered 34 campuses just 4 months after its launch. The advertising firm Y2M tried to convince Thefacebook team to expand to even larger universities, but Zuckerberg insisted that membership remain limited to students, staff, and graduates of Ivy League and other elite schools. Thefacebook took up much of Zuckerberg's free time, but he still thought of it as just one of several projects. In the meantime, he delved into yet another new venture. With his Phillips Exeter friend Adam D'Angelo and Harvard sophomore Andrew McCollum, he began developing

After his involvement with Facebook, Sean Parker invested in the music-streaming service Spotify and engineered a collaboration between Facebook and Spotify.

software that would allow users to exchange any kind of digital information, including music, video, photos, and text files. They named it Wirehog, and it would lead to new features and applications on a later version of Facebook.

Summer in Silicon Valley

Andrew McCollum had a summer 2004 internship at a video game company near Palo Alto, California. This Northern California city is within the region known as Silicon Valley, home to many of the world's largest technology corporations. Zuckerberg decided that the summer would be a good time to explore this area, particularly with McCollum being there and with Adam D'Angelo willing to join them. He used Craigslist to find a Silicon Valley house to rent for the summer. He recruited Moskovitz and two interns to join them. Using $15,000 of capital secured by Saverin, they all moved to a home at 819 La Jennifer Way in Palo Alto. Saverin decided not to go, electing to work in New York and seek out more advertisers there.

One day in early June 2004, Zuckerberg and his companions were carrying groceries back to their rented house in Palo Alto and ran into Sean Parker, the internet developer Zuckerberg had met in New York two months earlier. Parker's girlfriend happened to live just down the street from the house on La Jennifer Way. Upon hearing that Parker had lost about half of his shares in an internet company he had cofounded, Zuckerberg invited him to move into the house with the rest of Thefacebook team. Parker accepted, taking a room furnished with one bare mattress. He agreed to share his BMW with Zuckerberg and the other housemates. For a time, it was their only car.

Keeping Up with the Network

Thefacebook team's summer work consisted mostly of refining and shoring up the site for the upcoming semester. The website experienced a drop in traffic during the summer, when most college students were away from school, but Zuckerberg expected growth to pick up again in the fall. At the same time, Zuckerberg was not certain that Thefacebook would experience continued success. As Parker recounted, "He had these doubts. Was it a fad? Was it going to go away? He liked the idea of Thefacebook, and he was willing to pursue it doggedly, tenaciously, to the end. But like the best empire builders, he was both very determined and very skeptical."[40]

Where Is Silicon Valley?

The phrase "Silicon Valley" first appeared in January 1971 as part of a series of articles published in the weekly trade newspaper *Electronic News*. Journalist Don Hoefler coined the phrase to describe the high number of companies in the semiconductor and computer industries around the southern part of San Francisco Bay in California. Earlier in the 20th century, this region was also known for its innovators in the electronics industry, with Stanford University graduates and the U.S. Navy producing new radio, television, and military technologies. Encompassing several cities, including Palo Alto and San Jose, Silicon Valley is home to thousands of high-tech companies, including Apple, eBay, Google, Yahoo, Hewlett-Packard, and Facebook.

One of Zuckerberg's main concerns was keeping Thefacebook free of technical glitches. An online network could easily fail if it expanded too quickly and experienced service outages. This is what had happened to Friendster—it grew too fast and became clogged with users, causing the site to slow down and freeze up. This is one of the reasons that it eventually failed as a social network.

To avoid being "Friendstered," Zuckerberg and his team continually upgraded the database and reconfigured the servers in a way that enabled Thefacebook to hold 10 times more users than it had at the moment. In addition, Zuckerberg and Moskovitz carefully paced Thefacebook's growth. They would launch the website at a new campus, observe the initial surge in membership, and allow the traffic to slow down and level off. If they experienced technical difficulties or did not yet have the money to buy more server power, they would wait before adding another school. Thus, Thefacebook's expansion was methodical and deliberate. In Zuckerberg's words, "We didn't just go out and get a lot of investment and scale it. We kind of intentionally slowed it down at the beginning. We literally rolled it out school by school."[41]

An Intense Environment

The environment at the Palo Alto house was a quirky combination of dormitory, fraternity house, and computer lab. Zuckerberg and his team established a daily routine of sleeping late and then heading to work at the dining room table, which was crowded with computers, cables, modems—and bottles, cans, and food wrappers. As they programmed, no one talked. All communication occurred through their computers by instant messaging, even if they were sitting right next to one another. This helped them concentrate. Writer David Kirkpatrick noted, "Geeks like Zuckerberg and Moskovitz like to get deep into what is almost a trance when they're coding, and while they don't mind background music or the TV playing, they couldn't stand interruptions."[42]

Zuckerberg typically wore a T-shirt and pajamas for work. He slept later than most of the others, usually starting work in the afternoon and continuing late into the night. Although the interns did most of the tedious work, Zuckerberg sometimes stayed up all night, if necessary, to keep the system running. He also spent a lot of time refining Wirehog and programming other features for Thefacebook. Interestingly, neither Zuckerberg nor his summer team were themselves big users of Thefacebook. As they gathered information about its users, though, they learned that some people spent a lot of time on the website, looking through dozens of profiles each day. The team aimed to structure the site for this kind of user.

Sometimes the team would raucously discuss and debate ideas. When this happened, Zuckerberg paced back and forth around the dining room. He had brought his fencing equipment with him, and he liked to grab his foil, lunge, and slice it through the air as he made his points. Moskovitz did not appreciate this. "I'm the personality type where that would get [to] me sometimes," he explained. "But when he got into the mood he would do it for a couple of hours."[43] Eventually, the team banned Zuckerberg's indoor fencing.

Letting Loose

Zuckerberg and his friends did not spend all of their time working. Late at night, they took breaks to drink beer, watch movies, and play video games. Parker was the only one in the group who was over 21, so they relied on him to purchase alcohol. Sometimes he bought marijuana to share as well, but Zuckerberg would not smoke it.

The house had a pool in the backyard. McCollum strung a cable from the chimney on top of the house to a pole next to the pool, creating a zip line so that people could slide down from the roof and into the water. Thefacebook team liked to grill steaks and hang out poolside, drinking, swimming, and talking loudly late into the night. They sometimes used Thefacebook to announce house parties, attracting mobs of local young people and students from nearby Stanford University. Some people came over and hung out for several days.

Drunken antics led to broken furniture, broken bottles, and broken doors. Trash, barbecue ashes, and shards of glass often ended up in the pool, and neighbors complained about the late-night rowdiness.

Saverin Exits

Despite all the boisterous partying, Thefacebook was becoming a serious enterprise. Zuckerberg turned down a $10 million offer for Thefacebook in June 2004. With chief financial officer Saverin in New York drumming up advertisers, Zuckerberg began to rely more on Parker for advice on securing assets and expanding the business. Parker had experience in developing internet companies, as well as connections with investors. Parker also recognized that Thefacebook's LLC status would not be sufficient for a growing business, and he met with a lawyer to restructure the fledgling company.

With school out for the summer, Thefacebook's advertising sales slowed down. Zuckerberg needed money to buy new equipment and began using some of his own savings as well as contributions from his parents. In mid-June, Parker started meeting with investors about financing Thefacebook. Saverin became upset when he heard about this. He wrote a letter to Zuckerberg, arguing that the original agreement among the partners gave him control over Thefacebook's business strategies. He now demanded a contract to guarantee him that control.

Thus began a deep disagreement between Zuckerberg and Saverin. In Zuckerberg's opinion, Saverin was demanding to be chief executive officer (CEO) of Thefacebook without making a full-time commitment, as the other partners had. Moreover, as Zuckerberg explained in a legal filing, "Until [Saverin] had written authority to do what he wanted with the business, he would obstruct … the advancement of the business itself. … Since he owned 30 percent … he would make it impossible for the business to raise any financing until this matter was resolved."[44] For example, at one crucial moment, when Zuckerberg needed to purchase new servers, Saverin froze Thefacebook's bank account, refusing to release any money until his demands were met. That action required Zuckerberg and his parents to spend $85,000 of their own funds to keep Thefacebook running.

After Eduardo Saverin's experience with the early Facebook company, he became a venture capitalist and invested in more tech start-ups.

Saverin's demands were not entirely unreasonable. Early on, he had invested thousands of dollars in Thefacebook, and he had been meeting with advertisers to bring in revenue. This was often difficult work, and it was made more frustrating because Zuckerberg was nonchalant about revenue and preferred to keep ads to a minimum. As the two friends argued by phone and letter about their roles and responsibilities, Parker completed the legal negotiations that restructured Thefacebook as a corporation. Saverin retained some ownership but was eventually fired from the company. The new bylaws made Zuckerberg Thefacebook's sole director, with Parker as the company president.

More Money, More Demand

Along with negotiating Thefacebook's corporate status, Parker arranged for Zuckerberg to meet Peter Thiel, a cofounder of PayPal and a professional investor. Impressed with how quickly students were joining Thefacebook as soon as it became available at their campus, Thiel agreed to give the company a loan of $500,000.

It was just what Thefacebook needed. Membership had increased to 200,000, and Zuckerberg and his team needed to buy new servers to accommodate the growing demand. During the first week of the fall 2004 semester, they added 15 new colleges, and Thefacebook began to expand to larger universities and non–Ivy League schools.

Anticipating a very busy year for Thefacebook, Zuckerberg decided not to return to Harvard. Moskovitz and McCollum also elected to stay in Silicon Valley. Since they had to vacate the Palo Alto house, the remaining members of Thefacebook team moved to a new rental in Los Altos Hills. There would be no more complaints from neighbors about late-night rowdiness—this house, dubbed Casa Facebook, was right next to a busy interstate with traffic noise that blocked out other sounds.

Although Zuckerberg would never return to Harvard to finish his degree, the university awarded him an Honorary Doctor of Laws Degree in 2017.

Introducing the Wall

In September 2004, Zuckerberg introduced two new elements to Thefacebook. One, the Wall, allowed members to write comments and messages directly on other members' profiles. The comments would be visible to anyone who read a user's profile, and others could write responses to those comments

This screenshot shows Thefacebook as it looked in December 2004.

in their own posts to the Wall. The other addition, Groups, allowed a user to create a group based on any interest or topic. A Group could have its own page—similar to an individual's profile—complete with its own Wall where comments could be posted.

The Wall was especially popular. With the data they had gathered over the summer, Thefacebook team knew that people spent hours just looking through profiles on the website. Because it offered more information on members, the Wall increased this tendency for people to log in and linger on Thefacebook, wandering from profile to profile.

Thefacebook's membership grew rapidly. By the end of September 2004, it had reached 400,000, nearly doubling in a month. It had up to half a million members on October 21, then skyrocketed to 1 million members by November 30. By mid-February 2005, Thefacebook had 2 million active members at 370 colleges. Sixty-five percent of them were logging on daily, and ninety percent were returning to the site at least once a week. This phenomenal growth—from a handful of friends to 2 million members—occurred just 1 year after Thefacebook's dorm-room launch.

A Big Business Decision

Continued success for Thefacebook meant more employees, more equipment, and more cash were needed. That meant more investors—or at least an investor with a lot of money. Word about Thefacebook was getting around to more than college students. Venture capital firms and tech companies came knocking—some literally came to the house—to offer funds. However, Zuckerberg knew to be careful. He wanted to maintain control over the company, and many investors only offered money in exchange for power. A few made very convincing offers.

For example, an executive from the Viacom company offered to fly Zuckerberg home to New York for the holidays in a private jet. When Zuckerberg admired the plane, the executive told him he could buy his own plane if he sold just a piece of the business to Viacom. Zuckerberg would later be offered more than $800 million, but he claimed he did not need the money.

Early in 2005, Zuckerberg seriously considered an offer from Donald Graham, CEO of the Washington Post Company. Graham offered to invest $6 million in Thefacebook in return for 10-percent ownership. Zuckerberg unofficially agreed to the offer. However, soon after, a venture capital firm called Accel offered $12.7 million for just 11 percent of the company. Zuckerberg was torn. Accel was offering a much better deal, but he had given his word to Graham.

A coworker found Zuckerberg in tears, conflicted about the decision, and suggested he talk to Graham about the predicament. Graham was impressed that the young CEO had not just backed out of the deal. He released him from their informal agreement and wished him well. Zuckerberg, in turn, was so impressed with Graham's kindness that he later asked him to sit on Facebook's board of directors. The deal with Accel went through on May 26, 2005. Thefacebook finally had enough money to become the company that Zuckerberg wanted it to be—and he still retained control over it.

A Scary Encounter

On the same day the Accel deal was finalized, May 26, 2005, Zuckerberg drove his car to a gas station. He was on his way to celebrate with his girlfriend. While he was putting gas in the car, a man approached him with a gun and demanded money. Zuckerberg was very frightened. However, rather than give the man money or reason with him, he just jumped into his car and drove away. Luckily, the man did not shoot his gun. Zuckerberg felt shaken but lucky to be alive after that incident.

This was the Facebook logo used after the social network's name change. The font was altered slightly in 2015, but this original version is still used in some places.

On September 20, 2005, Thefacebook dropped "The" from its title and officially became Facebook. Sean Parker negotiated with AboutFace for the web address facebook.com. While AboutFace was not interested in Facebook's offer of stock as payment, it did accept Parker's payment of $200,000 in cash. The newly branded Facebook unveiled a new logo, a symbol of a new beginning.

Chapter **Four**

Learning on
the Job

By the fall of 2005, Mark Zuckerberg's nearly two-year-old social network had 5 million active users, a term that means the members who logged on at least once a month. Eighty-five percent of American college students had Facebook accounts. About 20,000 new users were joining each day. With the student market cornered, Zuckerberg and his partners began to think about ways to interest different populations in their social network.

Zuckerberg had a vision for Facebook—a vision that was becoming a reality. When people asked him to describe what Facebook was, he called it a "utility," similar to the way natural gas, electricity, and telephone companies are utilities. They provide basic and essential products. To Zuckerberg, his Facebook was a utility because it allowed people to connect, share information, and stay in touch. However, to truly be seen this way, and not as a fad or niche network, it would need to branch out from only connecting college students. The Facebook team was determined to reach new populations.

Parker Steps Down

Zuckerberg's first significant challenge with the newly named Facebook was dealing with Sean Parker, the company president. Parker was savvy about starting new internet companies, had a lot of connections in Silicon Valley, and had become a friend and trusted adviser. Yet Parker also had a reputation for partying, rebelliousness, and unpredictability. During a party he hosted in the late summer of 2005 while vacationing in North Carolina, Parker was arrested—though not formally charged—for possession of cocaine. He was quickly released and allowed to return to California.

Zuckerberg initially decided not to take any action in the wake of Parker's arrest. Since Parker had not been officially charged with a crime, Zuckerberg was not convinced any wrongdoing had occurred. However, board member Jim Breyer was very concerned when he learned about the incident. Breyer was the representative for Accel, the venture firm that had invested $12.7 million in Facebook. He knew about allegations of Parker's drug use and recklessness at his previous places of work. Also, rumor had it that an underage female employee was at the party when Parker was arrested. Breyer did not feel this was appropriate behavior for a president of Facebook. He insisted that Parker resign and threatened to file a lawsuit for not being immediately informed about Parker's arrest. After several days of negotiation and emotional discussions between Zuckerberg and Parker, Parker agreed to step down.

Branching Out

During the fall of 2005, Zuckerberg started allowing high school students to become members of Facebook. Some of the other Facebook executives disagreed with this idea at first, arguing that the college members would not want younger people coming into a network originally established for adults. If Facebook was to become a communications utility, however, it needed to compete with MySpace, a large

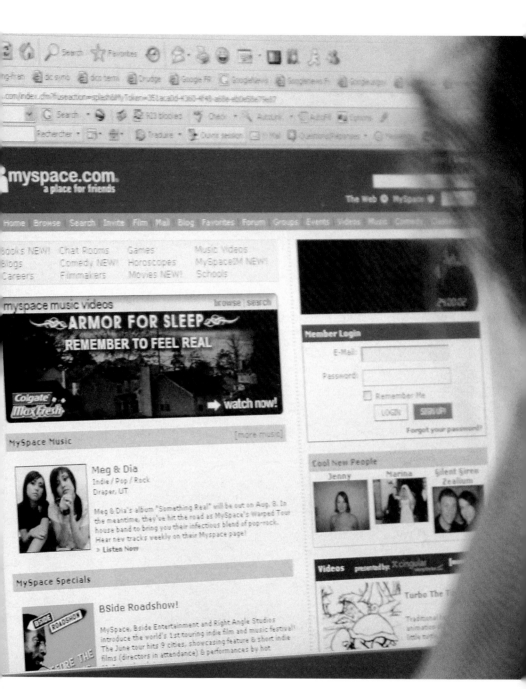

MySpace was created by Tom Anderson and Chris DeWolf in 2003, before Facebook was launched. It became a popular space for social networking and sharing and promoting music.

and growing social network that had become very popular with young people. As Breyer explained, "We knew that if we were going to win big, we had to start getting the hearts and minds of high schoolers."[45]

Facebook encouraged its college members to invite their friends who were still in high school. At first, high school members were limited to a separate Facebook, where they could not see the profiles of college members. In February 2006, the two Facebooks were merged, allowing members to connect with other users regardless of their age or grade, with the minimum age for membership set at 13. By April 2006, more than 1 million high school students had joined Facebook.

Other innovations continued to attract more members to Facebook. For example, Zuckerberg noticed that a lot of users enjoyed changing their profile photo—sometimes several times a day. Facebook's design at the time allowed just one photo per profile, so Zuckerberg enlisted his programmers to turn Facebook into a site where members could upload, share, and store multiple photos. In addition, members could identify, or tag, themselves and their friends in the photos. Photo sharing quickly became Facebook's most popular feature. Many members set up their profiles to receive email alerts when they were tagged in photos, and these alerts encouraged them to return to Facebook more often. Within a month of launching the photo hosting feature, 85 percent of Facebook members had been tagged in photos, and 70 percent were logging in to the website daily.

The News Feed Storm

Zuckerberg and his team introduced two more Facebook features, the News Feed and Mini-Feed, on September 5, 2006. The News Feed appeared on every user's home page, showing all the Facebook activities (posts, comments, added photos, etc.) of all the friends in one's network, while the Mini-Feed recorded one's activities on one's own Wall. These elements allowed members to easily track their friends' Facebook actions by the minute. No longer would people have to click on individual profiles or wander from one profile page to another to see what their friends had posted. All updates were available on their home page.

Complaints emerged immediately among Facebook's members. Many people felt that the News Feed edged too closely to violating privacy. A group called Students Against Facebook News Feed formed on Facebook, gathering more than 100,000 people in less than 24 hours and peaking at 750,000 members. These people contended that they did not want everyone in their network to know when and what they were updating all the time. Some of them called for sit-in protests at Facebook's headquarters in Palo Alto, and television news teams began gathering outside the offices. While demonstrations never materialized, the company hired security guards to help calm the nerves of frightened employees.

Zuckerberg was in New York on a business trip when this controversy erupted. Hoping to calm tensions by appealing to logic, he wrote a blog post clarifying that the News Feed had built-in protections: "None of your information is visible to anyone who couldn't see it before the changes."[46] This explanation did not satisfy Students Against Facebook News Feed, and it implied a lack of foresight and understanding on Zuckerberg's part. For one thing, the abrupt debut of a highly efficient feature caught many people off-guard. Even though information was shared only within one's network, users felt suddenly exposed, as if their updates were being broadcast publicly. While many people enjoyed sharing news and opinions with *some* friends in their network, they did not necessarily want *all* their friends to have quick access to everything they posted.

An Apology and a Revamp

In the end, Zuckerberg admitted that he and his team had erred: "We really messed this one up," he wrote to members in a follow-up post. "We did a bad job of explaining what the new features were and an even worse job of giving you control over them ... We didn't build in the proper privacy controls right away. This was a big mistake on our part, and I'm sorry for it."[47] Facebook's engineers quickly revamped the News Feed, allowing users more control over what activities were displayed to their network. The uproar against the News Feed did not totally disappear, but it quieted down significantly.

Interestingly, as angry as some people were about the News Feed, the anti-Feed protest had grown so fast because users heard about it through their own News Feeds. Members who claimed to hate the feature still used it, and people began spending even more time on Facebook than they had prior to the addition of the News Feed. Zuckerberg had the figures to prove this: In August 2006, members viewed 12 billion pages through Facebook. In October, after the addition of the News Feed, they viewed 22 billion pages.

The autumn of 2006 marked another important milestone for Facebook. On September 26, the network became open to anyone age 13 and over with a valid email address. Facebook was no longer a student-focused system, and new members—50,000 or more a day—began pouring in.

To Sell or Not to Sell

Facebook's rapid growth continued to attract offers from investors and major companies. Yahoo offered Zuckerberg $1 billion to purchase Facebook. Michael Wolf, president of MTV, offered $1.5 billion. A reputable source has said that Microsoft upped the ante even more, offering $15 billion. Feeling confident after the upsurge in Facebook membership, Zuckerberg turned them all down. He still had a vision for the growing network and was less interested in accruing wealth than in nurturing and molding a technically based social tool to make the world more open and connected. As Zuckerberg mentioned in a company mission statement, "We don't build services to make money; we make money to build better services. ... These days I think more and more people want to use services from companies that believe in something beyond simply maximizing profits."[48]

The Facebook Campus

The Facebook headquarters is located at 1 Hacker Way in Menlo Park, California. Employees were consulted on what kinds of interior design would make their workday more creative and productive. This led to the formation of indoor neighborhoods that give each department a unique style. Many employees work in open spaces, rather than in separate, walled-off cubicles.

The company provides three free meals a day, with snacks and beverages offered in mini-kitchens. Free laundry, board games, exercise areas, and relaxation lounges are also provided. Employees are encouraged to write on the walls, contribute artwork, and move furniture where they please. They can also bicycle and skateboard through the concrete-floored halls.

In 2018, about 15,000 employees worked for Facebook in Menlo Park. However, executives expect the number will grow to 35,000 by 2028.

Some board members and employees—about 150 total at the time—worried about Zuckerberg's decisions not to sell. He admitted these choices were not always easy for him to make, given that he was still quite young and learning how to do his job. In an interview on CNBC, Zuckerberg said, "The hardest [decision] was really when Yahoo offered us a billion dollars, because that was the first really big offer. At the time I knew nothing about business. I knew nothing about what a company could be worth, and I had to make this argument to people that somehow this was going to be the right decision."[49] Not everyone was persuaded, and some employees left the company. However, most stayed.

Facebook offers many benefits to its employees, including welcoming and attractive spaces in which to work.

In October 2007, Microsoft came back to Facebook with a different kind of offer: an investment of $240 million in return for only 1.6 percent of the company. Zuckerberg accepted this deal, which set Facebook's value at $15 billion. The agreement allowed Microsoft to serve as the provider for ads running on Facebook's U.S. site until 2011.

A Popular Platform

Part of what had prompted Microsoft's investment was Zuckerberg's decision to launch Facebook Platform, a systemic feature that enabled outside parties to create programs that work on Facebook. In other words, the website was reconfigured into a platform for applications, commonly referred to as "apps." Facebook would serve as a supportive environment in which any programmer could build and share tools. Within weeks of the May 2007 launch of Facebook Platform, many new apps were built, providing numerous tools that allowed members to personalize their profiles with links, images, music, and videos. A variety of popular social games, such as FarmVille and Mafia Wars, emerged as well. These new features attracted even more new members.

Back in 2004, Zuckerberg had created his own file-sharing program, Wirehog, but he had suspended it in 2006. By turning Facebook into a platform, Zuckerberg took the pressure off himself and his employees to create all the best new apps. As Zuckerberg explained at a conference in San Francisco,

> Companies like Microsoft or Google have tens of thousands of engineers. We're tiny compared to that. So ... how can we ever possibly build all the stuff that we want to see out there? The answer is to build an ecosystem and make it so that all these developers—whether it's a student in a dorm room who hasn't had a job yet, a big company, or a company that we've never heard of in some other country—can just build the stuff. And that's the part that's so cool about it.[50]

While their approaches differed from that of Facebook's, software giants Microsoft and Apple had also become successful by establishing their products as platforms. As it became obvious that millions were joining Facebook after its platform launch, Microsoft saw that the network was a good investment opportunity. In turn, Microsoft's investment was an enormous boost to Facebook, which had 50 million active members by October 2007. It gave Zuckerberg the resources to hire hundreds more employees, buy technology to keep up with accelerating growth, and expand internationally. Undoubtedly, Zuckerberg was developing entrepreneurial skills.

Invasion of Privacy?

Zuckerberg immediately launched more Facebook features after the Microsoft investment. On November 6, 2007, he hosted a gala for the New York advertising community, announcing that any commercial entity could create its own page on Facebook for free. A user could become a "fan" of these pages. When a member clicked the "become a fan" button (later, the Like button) on a page, it would be announced in their friends' News Feeds. It was a form of free advertising, but Zuckerberg also believed that it would encourage companies to purchase ad space once they saw the marketing possibilities. Facebook's online advertising potential was—and is—enormous, in part because it gathers information about its members. Details such as age, gender, musical tastes, hobbies, and so on can be used to place highly targeted ads.

Zuckerberg also introduced Beacon, a program that sent information about a member's purchases to their friends and to Facebook partner sites. It did this by tracking users' web-surfing habits, even when they were not logged in to Facebook. It also allowed Facebook's advertising partners to notify a user's friends when the user bought one of their products.

Beacon was a near disaster. Many members felt Facebook was invading their privacy to reap profits. Stories appeared in the press about people who had unintentionally announced their purchases to their friends on Facebook. A number of users found their entire Christmas gift list had been broadcast in the News Feed. Beacon even began to damage sales among some e-retailers, as people became reluctant to buy products through the internet out of fear that their personal information was no longer protected.

A Fatal Blow to Beacon

The backlash was immediate. Several activist groups, led by the political organization MoveOn, filed complaints with the Federal Trade Commission. Some groups initiated lawsuits. Facebook was heavily criticized in the news media, and the damage to its image was compounded because Zuckerberg remained silent about the controversy for three weeks.

Finally, Zuckerberg published an apologetic blog post on December 5, 2007. "We've made a lot of mistakes building this feature, but we've made even more with how we've handled them," he said. "We simply did a bad job with this release, and I apologize for it."[51] The solution was to allow Facebook users to turn Beacon off if they wished, and eventually, the feature was dropped. This satisfied some of the protest groups that had filed complaints, but negative feelings about Facebook lingered. Membership growth slowed down noticeably that winter. It picked up again in 2008, but in the years to come, as Facebook's privacy policies were repeatedly overhauled, many members found themselves frustrated and confused about how much control they had over the information they shared online.

As a result of the Beacon fiasco, board member Jim Breyer convinced Zuckerberg that Facebook needed a new chief operating officer (COO), someone experienced in public relations and online advertising. For this, they recruited Sheryl Sandberg, formerly a senior executive at Google. Zuckerberg remained CEO, but as COO, Sandberg would now provide guidance in developing stable and effective business strategies.

His Past Comes Back to Haunt Him

Zuckerberg soon faced some embarrassing privacy issues of his own. In connection with lawsuits filed in September 2004 and in March 2008 by ConnectU (originally Harvard Connection) creators Divya Narendra, Cameron Winklevoss, and Tyler Winklevoss, legal teams combed

Sheryl Sandberg has been Facebook's chief operating officer since 2008 and is credited with helping boost revenues for the social networking website.

In 2011, the Winklevoss brothers unsuccessfully argued in court that they should have received more in their 2008 settlement with Facebook.

through Zuckerberg's computer, seeking evidence related to the case. They came across dozens of emails and instant messages sent by Zuckerberg while he was still a student at Harvard, many of which revealed him to be mean-spirited and unethical. Together, they painted a very unflattering picture of Facebook's CEO.

For example, in a January 2004 message to his friend Adam D'Angelo, Zuckerberg wrote, "I'm making that dating site ... [It's] probably going to be released around the same time [as Thefacebook] ... Unless I [screw] the dating site over and quit on them right before I told them I'd have it done."[52] In a later response to a question about what he was going to do about the two competing projects, Zuckerberg cursed and implied he would intentionally damage the other site's chances of success. In yet another leaked exchange, Zuckerberg told a friend, "If you ever need any info about anyone at Harvard ... just ask ... I have over 4000 emails, pictures, addresses,

Another Settlement

Eduardo Saverin, the early Facebook investor, partner, and friend of Mark Zuckerberg, sued Zuckerberg and Thefacebook, claiming he had been unethically ejected from the company in 2005. Facebook settled the Saverin lawsuit for an undetermined amount and a 5-percent share in the company. He was also reinstated in the company roster as a cofounder. In an interview with *Forbes* magazine, Saverin stated, "I have only good things to say about Mark, there are no hard feelings between us. His focus on the company since its very first day is anything short of admirable."[1]

1. Quoted in Anderson Antunes, "Eduardo Saverin Finally Opens Up: 'No Hard Feelings Between Me and Mark Zuckerberg,'" *Forbes*, May 27, 2012.

sns [social security numbers]." When his friend asked why people had given him access to this data, Zuckerberg answered, "They 'trust me' ... dumb [idiots]."[53] In 2008, Facebook settled the lawsuit involving the Winklevoss brothers and Divya Narendra for Facebook shares that were valued at an estimated $65 million.

In a 2010 interview in the *New Yorker*, Zuckerberg stated that he "absolutely" regretted those messages. "If you're going to go on to build a service that is influential and that a lot of people rely on, then you need to be mature, right?" he said. "I think I've grown and learned a lot."[54] Zuckerberg's backers maintain he should not be judged by the antics he engaged in as a 19-year-old. One such supporter is Jim Breyer, who said, "After having a great deal of time with Mark, my confidence in him as C.E.O. of Facebook [is] in no way shaken. He is a brilliant individual who, like all of us, has made mistakes."[55]

Zuckerberg and The Social Network

Despite his mistakes, Zuckerberg had achieved phenomenal success by the end of 2010. In a mere six years, half a billion people had joined the website that he had launched from his computer in a messy dorm room. Facebook, with a continually changing mix of apps and features, was now the world's largest social network. *TIME* magazine named Mark Zuckerberg Person of the Year for 2010.

Zuckerberg's fame and wealth drew attention from the entertainment industry as well as the news media. In October 2010, *The Social Network*, a movie based on Zuckerberg's college years and the founding of Facebook, premiered. The screenplay was drawn from Ben Mezrich's 2009 book, *The Accidental Billionaires*. Mezrich based much of his work on interviews with former friends who had fallen out with Zuckerberg, such as Eduardo Saverin. Like the book, the film portrayed Zuckerberg as socially awkward, scheming, spiteful, and envious, although he was not an entirely unsympathetic character. Zuckerberg said that he believed parts of the movie to be unkind and some pure fiction. In an interview with

In the 2010 movie *The Social Network*, Jesse Eisenberg (center) portrayed Mark Zuckerberg, Justin Timberlake (left) portrayed Sean Parker, and Andrew Garfield (right) portrayed Eduardo Saverin.

ABC News, he said, "I mean, the real story is actually probably pretty boring, right? I mean, we just sat at our computers for six years and coded."[56] However, showing a more lighthearted version of himself, Zuckerberg made a surprise appearance on the comedy sketch show *Saturday Night Live* in January 2011. He joked with Jesse Eisenberg, the actor who had played him in *The Social Network*.

As the face of Facebook, Zuckerberg could not avoid the spotlight. Every major decision, mistake, and triumph was magnified in the press, but he faced it head-on. Even more challenges to Facebook's continued success were on the horizon.

Chapter **Five**

Facing Controversy with Facebook

On May 18, 2012, Facebook held its initial public offering (IPO), a process that allows the general public to buy stock in a company for the first time. Facebook offered over 421 million shares at a price of $38 per share, raising more than $16 billion. It was the largest technology IPO in U.S. history. Before the historic event, Mark Zuckerberg explained why Facebook was becoming a publicly traded company:

> We're going public for our employees and our investors. We made a commitment to them when we gave them equity that we'd work hard to make it worth a lot and make it liquid, and this IPO is fulfilling our commitment. As we become a public company, we're making a similar commitment to our new investors and we will work just as hard to fulfill it.[57]

Facebook "going public" meant that new stockholders had high expectations. They believed Facebook was an enterprise that could be relied upon to maintain its competitive edge—and they expected the values of their shares to keep going up. The social network sustained its growth after the IPO, thanks to Facebook's adoption in multiple countries,

Zuckerberg and other Facebook employees celebrated the company's IPO on May 18, 2012.

including India, Brazil, and Mexico. Plus, the Facebook mobile app and the Messenger instant-message service had made the social network more portable, convenient, and addictive to use than ever before.

Engaging Features

After the IPO, Zuckerberg and the Facebook team found new ways of making Facebook an indispensable part of the global community. Safety Check is a feature to aid Facebook members after an emergency situation such as a natural disaster or terrorist attack. First initiated in 2014, it is a quick way for users to tell others they are unharmed. Facebook activates the feature, determines a user's location, and sends a notification via smartphone asking if the user is safe. Choosing the "I'm Safe" button marks the user as safe, and all friends are notified. Zuckerberg described why Safety Check is important to the company: "How we judge whether Facebook is successful, it's not just on whether you can share a photo of a fun moment, . . . it's also whether our community is strong enough and we give people the tools to keep people safe in those situations."[58]

In 2016, Facebook Live offered a live-streaming service that could be used by businesses, organizations, and anyone interested in broadcasting their life rather than writing a post about it. Zuckerberg has even "gone live" on his

Facebook page to answer questions from users. People thought Live was fun, but it became controversial, too. It has been used to show crimes—even murders—in action. Anyone can post a video—no matter the content—and it may take hours for Facebook staff to find and remove videos that are violent or offensive.

Reaction buttons, introduced in 2016, are a popular feature that permit people to respond more expressively to posts as well as observe how others responded to their own. Facebook Marketplace also began in 2016, enabling users to buy and sell things more easily in their community—a service they might have used Craigslist for previously.

While the Like button, introduced in 2009, continues to be Facebook users' favorite button, many love being more expressive toward posts with the reaction buttons.

Acquisitions

Facebook, a company that so many had sought to acquire in its early years, has acquired several major applications and businesses itself. In 2012, it purchased the popular photo-sharing social network called Instagram for $1 billion. In 2014, it bought WhatsApp, a messaging app, for $16 million and about $12 million of Facebook stock. Also in 2014, Facebook purchased one of the first makers of virtual reality headsets: Oculus VR. Zuckerberg believes that virtual reality may host a social network in the future.

Zuckerberg believes there is a bright future for Oculus VR headsets (shown above).

Facebook ventured into the entertainment industry as well. Facebook Watch, a video-on-demand service, was announced in 2017, and Watch Party, first offered in 2018, allows people to watch videos together and chat about them.

A Look at His Life

Even while his company was constantly innovating, Zuckerberg's private life has not changed all that much. He has always stated that he is not interested in money but in connecting people and helping the world. Accordingly, beginning in 2013, he asked that his salary be set at $1, making him the lowest paid employee at Facebook. At the same time, Zuckerberg's net worth in 2018 was estimated to be about $56 billion because of his Facebook stock. He remains one of the richest people in the world.

Still, Zuckerberg maintains a low-key lifestyle. He prefers to wear gray T-shirts, jeans, flip-flops, and—in cool weather—fleece hoodies. He has been seen driving affordable cars such as an Acura, Volkswagen, and Honda. Driving is one of the activities that helps him relax, particularly after putting in 12 to 16 hours at the office or on the computer. He also practices meditation.

Zuckerberg sets yearly challenges to better himself. In 2010, for example, he began learning Mandarin Chinese. In 2011, he pledged to eat meat only from animals he had personally killed. He says the experience taught him about sustainable farming and how animals are raised. In 2012, he coded daily, while in 2013, he met someone new every day who does not work for Facebook. In 2014, Zuckerberg wrote a thank-you letter each day, and in 2015, he read a book every two weeks. The challenge of 2016 was to construct a "digital robot" to help at home, and in 2017, he visited all 50 U.S. states.

In January 2018, Zuckerberg's challenge was a bit different, and perhaps the most difficult of all. On his Facebook page, he wrote,

The world feels anxious and divided, and Facebook has a lot of work to do—whether it's protecting our community from abuse and hate, defending against interference by nation states, or making sure that time spent on Facebook is time well spent. My personal challenge for 2018 is to focus on fixing these important issues. We won't prevent all mistakes or abuse, but we currently make too many errors enforcing our policies and preventing misuse of our tools.[59]

Zuckerberg was reacting to a shocking discovery in 2017. Facebook had been used as a tool by Russians to influence the 2016 U.S. presidential election, a hotly contested race between Democrat Hillary Clinton and Republican Donald Trump.

Confronting Controversies

In September 2017, Facebook announced that about 3,000 election advertisements with connections to Russia had been purchased from 2015 to 2017. These were linked to around 470 fake accounts and pages. Most of the ads did not specifically mention the presidential election or the candidates. However, they focused on issues that divide people, such as gun rights and immigration. Facebook vice president of advertising Rob Goldman said the ads' purpose was to cause people to distrust the U.S. political system rather than to elect Trump, the eventual winner. He explained, "The main goal of the Russian propaganda and misinformation effort is to divide America by using our institutions, like free speech and social media, against us. It has stoked fear and hatred amongst Americans. It is working incredibly well."[60] It was estimated that about 10 million people saw these ads.

Because inauthentic accounts and pages—those that mislead others about identity and purpose—are in violation of Facebook's standards, they were removed from the platform. Facebook promised to block pages from advertising if they share false stories. In November 2017, Zuckerberg pledged to focus on security going forward, even noting that this focus could affect the company's profits: "I believe this will make our society stronger and in doing so will be good for all of us over the long term. But I want to be clear about what our priority is: Protecting our community is more important than maximizing our profits."[61]

However, a few months later, Facebook was at the center of another scandal. In March 2018, two newspapers, the *Guardian* and the *New York Times*, reported that data from more than 50 million Facebook profiles had been gathered by a research firm and sold to a company called Cambridge Analytica. When Facebook discovered that data had been transferred in 2015, violating its policies, the firm's app was banned, and both parties were told to delete the data. However, a cofounder of Cambridge Analytica, Christopher Wylie, claimed the data was not deleted. Instead, it was used to target people with pro-Trump messages before the 2016 election. Though Cambridge Analytica denied this, it was undeniable that people's private data had been sold—without their permission.

On March 25, 2018, Zuckerberg apologized in several major newspapers: "I'm sorry we didn't do more at the time. We're now taking steps to ensure this doesn't happen again."[62] He promised Facebook would start limiting the data that apps could acquire from users and would investigate all apps that were gathering large amounts of data.

In April 2018, Zuckerberg was called before the U.S. Congress to explain how Facebook handles users' data. He defended his company, but he also agreed that Facebook needed to take responsibility for what happened and be more vigilant about users' data going forward.

Giving Together

Amid the difficulties of his work, Zuckerberg's family has become a priority in his life and a refuge from the storm of controversies. He married his long-time girlfriend, Priscilla Chan, on May 19, 2012. They have two daughters: Maxima Chan Zuckerberg, born in 2015, and August Chan Zuckerberg, born in 2017. The family has used their considerable wealth in positive ways over the years.

Even before they married, Zuckerberg and Chan signed the Giving Pledge, a campaign that encourages the wealthiest

Data on Facebook

Aleksandr Kogan was the scientist who developed the app used to gather data for Cambridge Analytica. About 300,000 Facebook users were paid to download Kogan's app, called This Is Your Digital Life. They took surveys that helped Kogan collect information such as location, gender, birthday, "likes" on Facebook, and similar data about their friends as long as privacy settings allowed it. Kogan maintains that Facebook allowed this kind of data gathering at that time, and his actions were a common practice among app developers on the Facebook platform.

On the TV show *60 Minutes*, former Facebook employee Sandy Parakilas explained that Facebook uses people's data to make money. The company does not sell data, but it uses data to show ads it thinks the user will click on in their News Feed. He believes the Cambridge Analytica scandal happened because Facebook executives "prioritize the growth of users, the growth of the data they can collect and their ability to monetize that through advertising"[1] more than prioritizing privacy.

1. Quoted in Lesley Stahl, "Aleksander Kogan: The Link Between Cambridge Analytica and Facebook," *60 Minutes*, April 22, 2018.www.cbsnews.com/news/aleksandr-kogan-the -link-between-cambridge-analytica-and-facebook/.

Zuckerberg spoke in front of members of Congress in April 2018. He answered questions about how his company managed people's private data.

people in the United States to commit to donating at least half their lifetime earnings to charity. Other participants include Bill and Melinda Gates, George Lucas, and Zuckerberg's friend and Facebook cofounder Dustin Moskovitz. "People wait until late in their career to give back," Zuckerberg said in his pledge letter. "But why wait when there is so much to be done?"[63]

Zuckerberg and Chan took an even bolder step in December 2015, after the birth of their first child, Maxima, in establishing the Chan Zuckerberg Initiative (CZI). Through this organization, they promised to use 99 percent of their Facebook shares—worth about $45 billion—to focus on a wide range of critical issues, such as education, health care, affordable housing, immigration reform, and criminal justice reform. One example of CZI's efforts is its support of the Human

Zuckerberg and Chan visited the White House a few months before the birth of their first child in 2015.

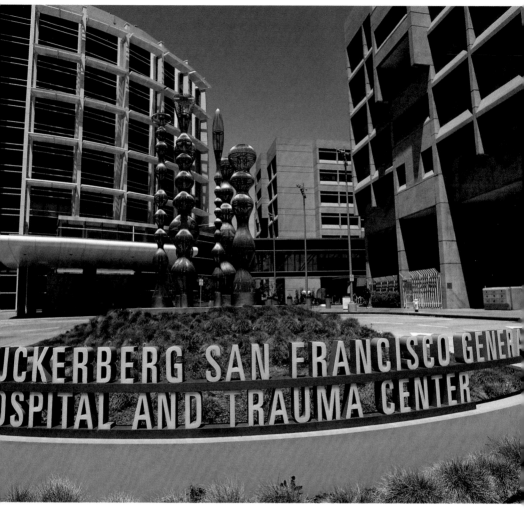

In 2011, Priscilla Chan and Mark Zuckerberg donated $75 million to San Francisco General Hospital—the largest private gift from individuals to a public hospital in the country. In recognition of this, the hospital changed its name.

Cell Atlas, a project to map out every cell in the human body. This would have a major impact on health care. In September 2016, CZI dedicated $3 billion to "cure all disease by the end of the century."[64] Recognizing that researchers are often only funded for short-term projects, this ambitious plan funds scientists whose promising research may take decades.

The Future of Facebook

Zuckerberg's philanthropy clearly shows his concerns about the future of the human race. However, the Facebook controversies of recent years have raised concerns about the future of the social network itself. Can users' data and privacy truly be protected? Will Facebook continue to be misused by people spreading misinformation? Should Facebook be regulated by the government or some other organization? Can Zuckerberg provide the leadership needed to address members' concerns?

In June 2018, Facebook's value dropped $119 billion in just one day. This was thought to be a consequence of the announcement that its user and revenue numbers were growing more slowly than normal. While Facebook's value did climb again, analysts wonder if the social network can keep reinventing itself to retain its place as a top technology company. Time will tell if it has become the indispensable "utility" that Zuckerberg wants it to be.

In many ways, Mark Zuckerberg is a study in contrasts. Journalists and colleagues have noted Zuckerberg's shy nature, while others talk about his confidence. According to interviewer Jose Antonio Vargas, he can be "a strange mixture of shy and cocky" and "condescending … but face to face he is often charming."[65] He is a billionaire who wears T-shirts and flip-flops, a private person who wants to make the world a more open place, and a hacker who sets the rules in his network.

Facebook mirrors its creator in its contrasts: a corporation that calls itself a community, a free service that "costs" users private data, and a tool wielded to connect as well as divide. However, Zuckerberg continues to be hopeful about Facebook's positive role in society. At the 2018 F8 Conference, Zuckerberg addressed the "real challenges" facing his company, but he said,

We need to keep that sense of optimism. We need to take a broader view of our responsibility. It's not enough to just build

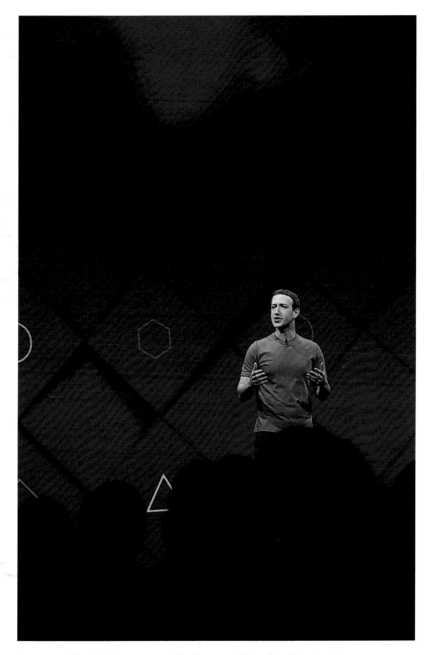

In 2017, Zuckerberg unveiled a new Facebook mission statement: "to bring the world closer together." While the Facebook community continues to expand, misuse of the platform has become a problem.

helpful, powerful tools. We need to make sure they are used for good. And we will.[66]

Zuckerberg's pledge to guide his social network into the future as an enduring force for good may be his greatest challenge yet.

Notes

Introduction: An Internet Architect

1. Quoted in Danielle Wiener-Bronner, "The 13 Best Lines from CNN's Mark Zuckerberg Interview," CNN Business, March 22, 2018. money.cnn.com/2018/03/22/news/companies/best-lines-zuckerberg-interview/index.html.

2. Quoted in Jeff Jarvis, *Public Parts: How Sharing in the Digital Age Improves the Way We Work and Live.* New York, NY: Simon and Schuster, 2011, p. 17.

3. Quoted in CNBC, *Mark Zuckerberg: Inside Facebook*, Documentary, January 26, 2012.

4. Quoted in Chris Sorenson, "Mark Zuckerberg: The Anti-Hero," *Maclean's*, December 13, 2010, p. 120.

5. Quoted in Sorenson, "Mark Zuckerberg: The Anti-Hero."

6. Quoted in CNBC, *Mark Zuckerberg: Inside Facebook*.

Chapter One: Growing Up Zuckerberg

7. Quoted in Nathaniel Popper, "Meet Edward Zuckerberg, Tech-Savvy Dentist (and Mark's Father)," *Los Angeles Times*, March 30, 2011. articles.latimes.com/2011/mar/30/business/la-fi-zuckerberg-father-20110330.

8. Quoted in Lev Grossman, "Person of the Year 2010: Mark Zuckerberg," *TIME*, December 15, 2010. www.time.com/time/specials/packages/article/0,28804,2036683_2037183_2037185,00.html.

9. Quoted in Beth J. Harpaz, "Mark Zuckerberg's Father Discusses Facebook CEO's Upbringing," *Huffington Post*, February 4, 2011. www.huffingtonpost.com/2011/02/04/mark-zuckerberg-father-edward_n_818892.html.

10. Quoted in Popper, "Meet Edward Zuckerberg, Tech-Savvy Dentist (and Mark's Father)."

11. Quoted in Harpaz, "Mark Zuckerberg's Father Discusses Facebook CEO's Upbringing."

12. Quoted in Jose Antonio Vargas, "The Face of Facebook," *New Yorker*, September 20, 2010. www.newyorker.com/reporting/2010/09/20/100920fa_fact_vargas.

13. Quoted in Vargas, "The Face of Facebook."

14. Quoted in Grossman, "Person of the Year 2010."

15. Quoted in Grossman, "Person of the Year 2010."

16. Quoted in Daniel Alef, *Mark Zuckerberg: The Face Behind Facebook and Social Networking*. Santa Barbara, CA: Titans of Fortune, 2010. Kindle edition.

17. Quoted in Claire Hoffman, "The Battle for Facebook," *Rolling Stone*, September 15, 2010. www.rollingstone.com/culture/news/the-battle-for-facebook-20100915.

18. Steffan Antonas, "Did Mark Zuckerberg's Inspiration for Facebook Come Before Harvard?," ReadWriteWeb, May 10, 2009. www.readwriteweb.com/archives/mark_zuckerberg_inspiration_for_facebook_before_harvard.php.

19. Antonas, "Did Mark Zuckerberg's Inspiration for Facebook Come Before Harvard?"

20. Quoted in Alef, *Mark Zuckerberg: The Face Behind Facebook and Social Networking*.

Chapter Two: Hacking at Harvard

21. David Kirkpatrick, *The Facebook Effect: The Inside Story of the Company That Is Connecting the World*. New York, NY: Simon and Schuster, 2010, p. 20.

22. Quoted in Vargas, "The Face of Facebook."

23. Quoted in Kirkpatrick, *The Facebook Effect*, p. 19.

24. Quoted in Kirkpatrick, *The Facebook Effect*, p. 26.

25. Quoted in Kirkpatrick, *The Facebook Effect*, p. 20.

26. Quoted in Ben Mezrich, *The Accidental Billionaires: The Founding of Facebook*. New York, NY: Anchor, 2009, p. 42.

27. Quoted in Mezrich, *The Accidental Billionaires*, p. 43.

28. Quoted in Mezrich, *The Accidental Billionaires*, p. 49.

29. Quoted in Bari M. Schwartz, "Hot or Not? Website Briefly Judges Looks," *Harvard Crimson*, November 4, 2003. www.thecrimson.com/article/2003/11/4/hot-or-not-website-briefly-judges.

30. Quoted in Kirkpatrick, *The Facebook Effect*, p. 25.

31. Quoted in Michael M. Grynbaum, "Mark E. Zuckerberg '06: The Whiz Behind Thefacebook.com," *Harvard Crimson*, June 10, 2004. dev.thecrimson.com/article/2004/6/10/mark-e-zuckerberg-06-the-whiz/.

32. Alan J. Tabak, "Hundreds Register for New Facebook Website," *Harvard Crimson*, February 9, 2004. www.thecrimson.com/article/2004/2/9/hundreds-register-for-new-facebook-website.

33. Quoted in Timothy J. McGinn, "Online Facebooks Duel Over Tangled Web of Authorship," *Harvard Crimson*, May 28, 2004. www.thecrimson.com/article/2004/5/28/online-facebooks-duel-over-tangled-web.

34. Quoted in McGinn, "Online Facebooks Duel Over Tangled Web of Authorship."

35. Quoted in Nicholas Carson, "At Last—the Full Story of How Facebook Was Founded," *Business Insider*, March 5, 2010. www.businessinsider.com/how-facebook-was-founded-2010-3.

36. Quoted in Hoffman, "The Battle for Facebook."

37. Quoted in Hoffman, "The Battle for Facebook."

Chapter Three: The Foundations of Facebook

38. Quoted in Alef, *Mark Zuckerberg: The Face Behind Facebook and Social Networking*.

39. Quoted in Kirkpatrick, *The Facebook Effect*, p. 47.

40. Quoted in Kirkpatrick, *The Facebook Effect*, p. 53.

41. Quoted in Kirkpatrick, *The Facebook Effect*, p. 58.

42. Kirkpatrick, *The Facebook Effect*, p. 49.

43. Quoted in Kirkpatrick, *The Facebook Effect*, p. 52.

44. Quoted in Kirkpatrick, *The Facebook Effect*, p. 60.

Chapter Four: Learning on the Job

45. Quoted in Kirkpatrick, *The Facebook Effect*, p. 149.

46. Quoted in Brittney Farb, "Students Speak Out Against Facebook Feed," *Student Life*, September 8, 2006. www.studlife.com/archives/News/2006/09/08/StudentsspeakoutagainstFacebookfeed.

47. Quoted in Kirkpatrick, *The Facebook Effect*, pp. 191–192.

48. Quoted in U.S. Securities and Exchange Commission. Form S-1 Registration Statement. February 1, 2012. www.sec.gov/Archives/edgar/data/1326801/000119312512034517/d287954ds1.htm.

49. Quoted in CNBC, *Mark Zuckerberg: Inside Facebook*.

50. Quoted in CNBC, *Mark Zuckerberg: Inside Facebook*.

51. Mark Zuckerberg, "Thoughts on Beacon," *The Facebook Blog*, December 6, 2007. blog.facebook.com/blog.php%3Fpost%3D7584397130.

52. Quoted in Carson, "At Last—the Full Story of How Facebook Was Founded."

53. Quoted in Vargas, "The Face of Facebook."

54. Quoted in Vargas, "The Face of Facebook."

55. Quoted in Vargas, "The Face of Facebook."

56. Quoted in Ki Mae Heussner, "Facebook CEO Mark Zuckerberg Talks to Diane Sawyer as Website Gets 500-Millionth Member," ABC News, July 21, 2010. abcnews.go.com/WN/zuckerberg-calls-movie-fiction-disputes-signing-contract-giving/story?id=11217015.

Chapter Five: Facing Controversy with Facebook

57. Quoted in Gerry Shih, "Zuckerberg's Letter to Investors," Reuters Business News, February 1, 2012. www.reuters.com/article/us-facebook-letter-idUSTRE8102MT20120201.

58. Quoted in Susmita Baral, "What Is Facebook Safety Check? Users Will Soon Be Able to Activate Feature to Alert Friends During Emergencies," *International Business Times*, August 29, 2016. www.ibtimes.com/what-facebook-safety-check-users-will-soon-be-able-activate-feature-alert-friends-2408810.

59. Mark Zuckerberg, Mark Zuckerberg's Facebook Page, January 4, 2018. www.facebook.com/zuck/posts/101043801707 14571?pnref=story.

60. Quoted in Hannah Kuchler, "Facebook Says Russia's Main Goal Is to Divide US," *Financial Times*, February 18, 2018. www.ft.com/content/f681fed6-144f-11e8-9376-4a6390addb44.

61. Quoted in Kurt Wagner, "Mark Zuckerberg Didn't Testify to Congress on Russia, But Says He's 'Dead Serious' About Fixing Things," Recode, November 1, 2017. www.recode.net/2017/11/1/16595334/mark-zuckerberg-congress-russia-profits-election-russia.

62. Quoted in Sheena McKenzie, "Facebook's Mark Zuckerberg Says Sorry in Full-Page Newspaper Ads," CNN, March 25, 2018. www.cnn.com/2018/03/25/europe/facebook-zuckerberg-cambridge-analytica-sorry-ads-newspapers-intl/index.html.

63. Quoted in Terje Langland, "Facebook's Zuckerberg Joins Gates, Buffett in Charity Pledge," *Washington Post*, December 9, 2010. www.washingtonpost.com/wp-dyn/content/article/2010/12/09/AR2010120900467.html?noredirect=on.

64. Quoted in Tess Townsend, "Mark Zuckerberg Wants to Cure All Disease by the End of the Century," *Inc.*, April 27, 2016. www.inc.com/tess-townsend/mark-zuckerberg-wants-to-cure-all-disease.html.

65. Vargas, "The Face of Facebook."

66. Quoted in Julie Bort, "Mark Zuckerberg Gave an Impassioned, Obama-like Speech Defending Facebook," *Business Insider*, May 1, 2018. www.businessinsider.com/mark-zuckerberg-gives-obama-like-speech-defending-facebook-2018-5.

Mark Zuckerberg Year by Year

1984

Mark Elliot Zuckerberg is born on May 14 to Edward and Karen Zuckerberg.

1995

Zuckerberg receives tutoring in computer programming from a software developer. He takes graduate level computer courses at Mercy College.

1996

Zuckerberg creates ZuckNet, a messaging program connecting computers in the Zuckerberg household.

1998

Zuckerberg attends Ardsley High School, where he excels in classics.

2000

Zuckerberg transfers to Phillips Exeter Academy.

2002

With Adam D'Angelo, Zuckerberg develops Synapse Media Player and turns down companies' offers of millions of dollars for it. He graduates from Phillips Exeter and enters Harvard University.

2003

Zuckerberg creates Course Match. He hacks the Harvard computer system and uses data to create Facemash. He is approached by Divya Narendra, Tyler Winklevoss, and Cameron Winklevoss to write code for Harvard Connection.

2004

Zuckerberg launches Thefacebook from his dorm room. He forms Thefacebook LLC as a partnership with Eduardo Saverin and Dustin Moskovitz and moves to Silicon Valley. Narendra and the Winklevoss brothers sue Thefacebook. Thefacebook's membership reaches 1 million.

2005

Zuckerberg fires Saverin. Accel Partners invests $12.7 million in Thefacebook. Thefacebook becomes Facebook, and its membership reaches 5 million.

2006

Facebook membership is opened to anyone with an email address. News Feed is launched.

2007

Zuckerberg launches Facebook Platform. Microsoft invests $240 million in Facebook. Facebook's membership grows to more than 50 million. Zuckerberg launches Beacon.

2008

Facebook settles Narendra and the Winklevoss brothers' lawsuit for an estimated $65 million.

2009

The Like button is introduced to Facebook members. Beacon is deactivated.

2010

Facebook's membership reaches more than 500 million. *The Social Network* film is released. Zuckerberg is named *TIME* magazine's Person of the Year. He signs the Giving Pledge, promising to donate most of his lifetime earnings to charity.

2011

Zuckerberg makes a surprise appearance on *Saturday Night Live*. Facebook's membership reaches 845 million in December.

2012

Facebook buys photo-sharing social network Instagram for $1 billion. Facebook holds an initial public offering, raising more than $16 billion. Zuckerberg marries Priscilla Chan on May 19.

2013

Zuckerberg's salary is set at $1 at his request, yet he remains one of the richest people in the world because of his Facebook stock.

2014

Facebook buys the messaging app WhatsApp and virtual reality headset maker Oculus VR.

2015

Zuckerberg's daughter Maxima Chan Zuckerberg is born in November. Zuckerberg and Chan launch the Chan Zuckerberg Initiative (CZI), promising to sell 99 percent of their Facebook shares to solve problems around the world.

2016

Reaction buttons are introduced to Facebook. CZI dedicates $3 billion to "cure all disease" by the end of the 21st century. Facebook's Marketplace allows people to buy and sell goods in their community.

2017

Zuckerberg's daughter August Chan Zuckerberg is born in August. Facebook announces that Russian-backed ads and pages were used to interfere with the 2016 U.S. presidential election. Zuckerberg promises to crack down on fake accounts.

2018

Facebook admits political data firm Cambridge Analytica accessed up to 87 million users' data. Zuckerberg testifies before Congress about how data is used. He promises Facebook will protect data better. Facebook reports 2.27 billion active users.

For More Information

Books

Beahm, George W., ed. *Mark Zuckerberg: In His Own Words*. Chicago, IL: B2 Books, 2018.
Read quotes from Mark Zuckerberg about many issues, including technology and his personal life.

Doak, Robin S. *Mark Zuckerberg*. New York, NY: Children's Press, 2016.
Find out how Zuckerberg turned Facebook into a billion-dollar business.

Hill, Z. B. *Mark Zuckerberg: From Facebook to Famous*. Broomall, PA: Mason Crest Publishers, 2013.
This book covers many details about Zuckerberg's early career at Facebook.

Kawa, Katie. *Mark Zuckerberg: Founder of Facebook*. New York, NY: PowerKids Press, 2017.
Discover how Zuckerberg's work has shaped our world and the way people use computers.

Sorensen, Lita. *Mark Zuckerberg and Priscilla Chan: Top Couple in Tech and Philanthropy*. New York, NY: Enslow Publishing, 2019.
Read more about how Zuckerberg and Chan are trying to change the world for the better.

Websites

Bloomberg Billionaires Index
(www.bloomberg.com/billionaires/profiles/mark-e-zuckerberg)
Find out where Zuckerberg is found on this list of billionaires.

Facebook Newsroom
(newsroom.fb.com)
Facebook employees give firsthand accounts of new features, products, and news at the company.

***Forbes*: Facebook**
(forbes.com/companies/facebook/#127ebdaf4193)
Read the latest Facebook numbers, such as its stock price and number of employees.

The Harvard Crimson
(www.thecrimson.com/)
Search for stories about Zuckerberg when he was a student at Harvard on the university's newspaper website.

Mark Zuckerberg
(www.investopedia.com/terms/m/mark-zuckerberg.asp)
Read a short biography of the Facebook CEO.

Index

Olson, Billy, 25, 28, 30, 32

Picture Credits

About the Author

Therese Harasymiw is an editor and author of over 300 children's books. She has written many books on hot topics in technology, including robotics, space tech, Lego Mindstorms, gamification, and cyberbullying, as well as a biography of Apple cofounder Steve Jobs. She holds degrees in English from Providence College and English education from the State University of New York at Buffalo. She currently lives in Rochester, New York, with her husband, Mark, and children, Luke and Martin.